ENVY THE FRIGHTENED

by Yaël Dayan

NEW FACE IN THE MIRROR

ENVY THE FRIGHTENED

YAËL DAYAN

# Envy
# the
# Frightened

THE WORLD PUBLISHING COMPANY

CLEVELAND AND NEW YORK

Published by The World Publishing Company
2231 West 110 Street, Cleveland 2, Ohio


Library of Congress Catalog Card Number: 60-11453

FIRST EDITION

To Udi and Assi my brothers

*Happy is the man who feareth alway . . .*

PROVERBS 28:14

# 1

WHEN the villagers discovered the secret place, and began to stroll by it, it was necessary to find a new one. And what better place could there be for meetings than the old cemetery?

The old place had been white, a small bare white valley where the beams of the sun were reflected from the rocks, and, finding no obstacle, shone on the white rocks opposite them. It seemed almost as if the rocks were sending messages back and forth across the uncovered heads of the serious group of children from Beit-On. The new place was gray, a weedy patch of soil among the tombstones and gray-green rocks on the upper slope of Cemetery Hill.

During the hot summer the children of Beit-On went to the lake to swim. Winter was storytelling and stamp collecting time. Spring, and it was spring now, was reserved for "Who is strong?" the secret game played in the secret meeting place.

Udi, the son of the village truck driver, was the leader

of the group. And when the boys sat tense and ready, afraid to move or talk, he would get up, hands in his pockets, and would ask the question, "Who is strong?"

Fast furtive sidewise glances, nervous little hands playing with stones, restless whispers, bare feet digging in the soil—then lowered eyes, and complete attention: it seemed for a moment as if the trees and the tombstones and the Galilean hills around, and the Lake of Tiberias below, had frozen and waited with Udi and Nimrod and Igal— And then one would get up—"*I* am strong!" he would say. The tension would break, and the game would go on, the children's chorus nervous but loud, almost a shout echoing through the demanding, teasing, challenging "Show us you're strong!"

And the lake, and hills and the ugly yellow tombstones would seem to come to life and join the chorus in whisper and rustle and shudder. "Show us you're strong," they too seemed to be saying. And show they would. And that's why you could see Udi walking one night, a dark one at that, among the hills; that's how Moti broke his leg climbing the weak tall tree in the white valley; that's how Udi finally became the leader by jumping down from the cliff without being hurt.

This was the aim of the game, to show that you could do what even you didn't believe you could do. It was a springtime game, and every spring the children of Beit-On jumped from the cliffs or climbed the trees or swam in the deepest part of the lake. And every spring, as the children grew up, the targets became harder to achieve. Leaders changed, meeting places were changed when discovered by others, and when it wasn't the tombstones, it was the caves near the stream, or the bees in the muddy swamp, or the trees in Kings Forest, that joined in saying: "Show us you're strong."

Nimrod was eight and lived in a whitewashed house in Beit-On. And as all houses of Beit-On looked alike it could be identified only by the broken cart in the yard opposite the house. He was well built and strong, sunburned and dark, and his hair was curly. This was a handicap as the boys used to tease him and call him girlish names. When he broke his leg one spring they stopped teasing him, but still he wished his hair was short and straight like Udi's.

This spring evening he came home late. It was in the afternoon that he had climbed the tree, and he couldn't tell anybody that he almost hadn't. His hands had been sweaty and his feet cold, and he had had the feeling that if stopped for a moment his legs wouldn't hold up. He dared not look down or up, and he saw only the trunk opposite him and heard only the whispers of the boys below. He tried not to think at all. He just went up the tree and then climbed down, and left the group to go home. Should he go to Lamech, he wondered, and tell him that he had been afraid, and what would Lamech say, being so old and wise, and making shoes for the villagers and sandals for the children.

He didn't go to Lamech but walked home, thinking, silent.

His father was out with the milk cart, and his mother was preparing supper. He approached her and his hands clung to her big waist and apron. She held him tight for a moment and then pushed him away. "Go wash, boy. Father will be back any moment."

"Mother," he said—and then stopped. No, he couldn't tell her. He threw his sandals in a corner, and when he washed he felt his palms burning and he hated the tree and the meeting place, and he washed his face so that he could hide his tears as he knew he shouldn't cry, and went back to the small kitchen. His mother looked at him, brushed back the curls, and casually asked, "Anything the matter, Nimi?"

"Don't call him Nimi," his father said, coming in the door. "That's my grown-up young man! He doesn't want to be nick-named any more!"

Nimrod lowered his head. He knew he shouldn't cry and he could think of no excuse to leave the room. His father, tall and slim, his khaki clothes almost hanging on him, went to the bathroom to wash before supper, singing to himself, and his mother nervously fiddled with the dishes.

He quickly rubbed his nose, taking the occasion to dry his tears, and thought of Lamech in his cottage where there was no electric light and it was rather dirty but cozy. He thought of the shapes of funny unknown animals formed by the scraps of leather on Lamech's floor, and he knew he shouldn't talk about this afternoon, anyway not about the way he had felt.

"I climbed the highest tree today, we played a game," he said, in a matter-of-fact voice.

"You weren't hurt, Nimi?" asked his mother.

"Nimrod," said Ivri, his father, "is a strong boy, so why would he be hurt? And he's not afraid. Remember when I sent him with a message to Gideon the other night and he wasn't afraid though it was dark and cold? Next year, Nimrod son, you'll climb a higher tree."

"There is no higher tree," said Nimrod. He was eating

his omelet, and he thought that there couldn't be a higher tree, and if there was one he didn't want to climb it, and next year he wouldn't jump from a higher cliff, or swim in deeper waters. He also thought he didn't like the feeling in his stomach when he had to do these things.

"Come for a walk, Miriam? Nimrod?"

He liked to walk after supper with Ivri. They would talk about the farm, and Ivri would tell him stories about Russia where he came from, and about his grandfather's shop and the snow, and sometimes they'd pass near Lamech's place and Nimrod would imagine the old man reading in the light of the oil lamp and would think about going there the next day to listen to stories, because Lamech, and he know this, was the best storyteller in Beit-On or maybe in the whole of Israel; he wouldn't say it, but maybe in the whole world.

"Did you climb high trees when you were eight, father?"

"No, Nimrod. They wouldn't let us. They thought Jewish boys should remain in their fathers' shops and not climb trees."

"Would you have been afraid to climb them?"

"No, son. And you're not afraid, are you? You remember when I sent you to Gideon with the message the other night and you weren't afraid?"

"I'm not. What shall I get for my birthday next month?"

"That's a secret! I'll get you something you'll keep all your life. Being nine is very important and next year you can help me with the cows."

Their long slim shadows disappeared as it grew darker. Ivri stopped to talk to other farmers, and Nimrod had so many questions to ask that he kept forgetting them. The mountain on the other side of the lake had a white cap on it. It was snow like that in his father's village, but it was far away. Not even in "Who is strong?" would the boys suggest that they go there.

They passed near the village synagogue. Nimrod never went in there. Lamech had said he would take him.

"Father, have you ever been in there?"

"No, son. I went to the synagogue when I was young, but my father made me go. We were dressed in little suits like some men you saw in Haifa when we went there, and we had to pray to God, and the Russian children mocked us. Don't be afraid, you needn't go. Some old men in Beit-On do, but not little children."

"I'm not afraid." Nimrod thought it would be amusing to be dressed in a little suit like the men in Haifa, and wondered if Lamech was once dressed like this. He couldn't imagine old, bearded, slightly dirty Lamech dressed in a neat suit, or in anything but his greasy apron and gray overalls.

And while he was thinking about this they passed through the center of the village, and the arms store on the path to the left, and through the small forest behind which you could already see the light from Lamech's house.

"Can we go in and see what Lamech is doing?"

"No, Nimrod, we'll go home now and listen to the news, and you will go to bed. You can't like Lamech, he's a silly old man, like the men in my Russian village. I've wondered why he didn't stay behind. He hasn't changed. And all these stories he feeds you with! If you like stories I can tell you some."

Nimrod didn't answer. He didn't like his father's stories much, for they were all the same, but it was better than no stories, especially after this afternoon.

"Yes, Father, I'd like you to tell me a story tonight."

"Not tonight, son, some other day. Tonight will be late

and we have a meeting. You go to sleep and think of yourself on the top of the high tree, and you'll sleep well."

Miriam was mending some socks in the kitchen which
looked clean and washed. She still had her apron on and
looked weary and detached. The radio was just broad-
casting the news and Ivri kissed his son on the top of his
head and sent him to bed. Miriam watched him folding
his shorts and undershirt and thought, once again, how
odd it would be when this little warm brown body would
be tall and grown and shy, and how odd he had looked
years ago when she came back with him from the hospital
to the village of Beit-On.

Nimrod pulled the sheet above his head. He tried to
think how it had felt up on top of the highest tree, but he
couldn't because all he remembered was climbing up,
and his hands burning, and being afraid to pause for a
moment or to look up or down, and climbing down and
going away. He thought it didn't feel like anything, and
wondered again whether Lamech would take him to pray,
and what kind of story his father would tell him some
other day, as he had promised. Above his bed was an old
sword his father had got from a Bedouin, and on the cupboard in a locked box a gun which he was allowed to look
at on Saturdays.

In the corner were piled some toy jeeps and a small model
of a cannon, and he didn't feel at all like saying good night
to any of these.

But, as it was a spring night, he could hear the birds,
and he smiled to them in the dark. Orange blossom, the
strongest of smells, filled the little room and put him to
sleep.

# 2

IVRI and Miriam were seated on the balcony, sipping tea from glasses and listening to the broadcast. They didn't talk much. Ivri was always tired, weary, and worried. He reached his arm across toward Miriam and touched her sunburned, tough, almost rough hand.

"I love Nimrod," Ivri said, "but he worries me."

"But he is only a boy."

"It isn't that. We have to turn him into a man. I don't want him to be like I was in my village."

"But he won't be. We're at home here."

"He should be more than that. And as he's only a child we can turn him into the person he should be. He should know no fears, he should be strong and friendly and self-sufficient. I want him in the first line, I want him"—he talked slowly, and Miriam wondered whether he even noticed that she was there at all—"I want him to be everything that's good and needed in this country and that we didn't have. I was scared when I was a child. I was afraid of the Cheder's teacher, afraid of the Russian children, of

the village policeman, afraid of my parents. I was afraid
of God, of the Rabbi, afraid of the look of foreigners and
even of nature. Nimrod will not fear a thing. I'll take him
with me on walks and trips. He'll learn to be superior, he'll
learn to be independent, learn to be alone." He spoke
faster, his hand nervously stroking Miriam's arm as if not
sure of what he was saying. "I'll teach him. I want to be
proud of him. I want him to be like Gideon."

"That fool. "

"Better than a silly old hag like Lamech. Gideon is a
hero, he fears nothing, he's strong, he's a new kind of man
here. I wish Nimrod would go to him and listen to his
stories instead of to a shoemaker."

"But, Ivri, your own father was a small shop owner. You
can't just rub out the past and history. Nimrod is a little
boy, let him be as he is, he'll be good enough for anything."
And thinking to herself she added, "I don't think you can
inject courage into anybody."

"One can. I will."

Ivri got up and went to the boy's room. He straightened
the sheet, straightened the old rusty sword on the wall, and
went out with his thoughts and plans to a meeting.


"Why doesn't Father like you, Lamech?" Nimrod was
sitting on a small stool, playing with pieces of leather, and
Lamech didn't answer for a while. He was short and slim
and very old; he hardly ever left his cottage, or if he did
people didn't see him in the village center too often.

"Little boy," he finally said, "many people don't like
others, not because they really don't but because they
think they shouldn't. I knew your grandfather. He liked
me. Maybe that's why your father doesn't. Little boy,
when is your birthday?"

"You'll give me a gift?"

"Yes, Nimrod, we'll make a nice leather toy. Now let's see. Would you like a cat with a long tail? Or would you like a funny donkey?" Old Lamech put his fingers near his gray head to imitate a donkey and smiled. When he smiled Nimrod used to wonder how he could eat without teeth. "Or—let's see! No, it'll be a surprise, I'll make you a special toy."

"I think I'd like a special toy. Now tell me more about God." It was in the afternoon, and Nimrod decided he wouldn't go to the secret meeting place. He didn't tell Lamech about climbing the tree because Lamech wouldn't have liked the story, he thought.

And Lamech talked about God. He talked about things which Nimrod didn't understand very well. He said that God wasn't like us, and that He was above somewhere, and that we were destined to follow His will. But we had to choose between good and evil, and this was His gift to us, choice, and we were doomed to choose, every moment, every year, and the result of our many decisions made God know how good or bad we were.

"What happens when we are bad?"

"We are punished, but it isn't a punishment we notice. We suffer, we regret, we step downward on the ladder of morals, happiness, and self-respect. And that's the punishment. And then one day we are at the bottom of the ladder, and the ladder disappears, and we can't go up any more."

"Am I good, Lamech? Can I be good?" Nimrod didn't like the dark idea of going down to some depth without having a way of climbing up again.

"You will be good if you love, because love of all enables us to compromise, to fear our God, and to know ourselves

as we are. You should love yourself Nimrod, and everything around you, as it was all created by God and it deserves our love. You love me, don't you?"

Nimrod said yes. It wasn't the first time Lamech asked
him that, and he wondered why he asked. He always said
yes but he wasn't sure whether he really loved Lamech.
He knew he loved his parents and the lake but he said
yes when Lamech asked him that.

"You are my only friend, Nimrod. I am, as your father
says, a silly old man, but you," and he took him and lifted
him—when you looked at Lamech you wouldn't believe
he could—and made him stand on the stool, "you have
the sun in you, and the fresh air." He stroked his bare
shoulders and arms and smiled a toothless smile. "And
you'll be full of love. Come for a walk?"

This was unusual. Never before had Lamech taken
Nimrod for a walk, and Nimrod couldn't disguise his surprise. "Yes!" he exclaimed, "let's!" Lamech took off his
apron—it was the first time that Nimrod had seen him
without it—and they went out. Nimrod thought it would
be nice to show Lamech the secret meeting place, as he
knew the children wouldn't be there now, so they climbed
Cemetery Hill, hand in hand, toward the evening.

When they passed near the tombs Nimrod noticed
Lamech's lips murmuring something.

"Did you say anything?"

"Yes, little boy. I was saying may they rest in peace, the
dead ones."

Nimrod thought very often about what was happening
under the tombstones, but he didn't want to ask about it
now. So he told Lamech about the trip his father would
take with him, to the high mountains. They would climb
at night to watch the sun rising at dawn.

Lamech clutched his hand so it almost hurt. He was breathing heavily trying to follow Nimrod's quick young steps.

He stopped. "I'm tired," he said. "Let us sit and watch the lake."

"Why don't you ever go out, Lamech? Don't you like it outside?"

"I do go out," and he bent toward Nimrod and whispered to him, "at night! I can even dance then. And I rejoice when I dance, and I sing our old songs, and I talk to the birds and to God."

"Does He talk back to you?"

"Well, not often. Sometimes. Actually only once. You see, all these"—and he stretched his arm toward the lake and the mountains—"were done by God and I love it, and love God with it. And then I dance and sing to Him, and that's like doing a good deed." Nimrod didn't understand it. He thought it must be very funny to see Lamech dancing at night on the hill with his smile and beard and gray hair and dirty trousers. But he knew he shouldn't laugh, even though he felt like it.

Lamech looked at him again when he stood up, and touched his strong legs and feet. "You're life, you see. I'm half in this cemetery!" He laughed and drew Nimrod close to him. "Don't be sad. I'll die one day, soon, and when you'll come here you'll pass near my tomb and you'll think of me. We are friends, aren't we?"

"Yes, we're friends. I have to go home now. Mother will be angry if I'm late for supper. Coming?"

"No. I'll stay here. This is my place. You run home, little one. Come over and we'll make toys."

"What toy will you give me for my birthday?"

"That's a secret!"

Nimrod didn't look back as he ran down the path toward the village. He could imagine Lamech standing there, and wondered whether he had started dancing and singing already. He didn't want to think about him like that. Actually he hadn't liked the walk with Lamech very much. He preferred to sit with him in the cottage and listen to stories and play with the leather bits. Lamech didn't look very well in the sun. He thought about the walk with his father, greeting the other farmers when they passed by, and about Lamech saying he'd be dead soon and under one of the ugly yellow tombstones.

He was late to supper. He knew it because his mother called him Nimrod instead of Nimi, and his father didn't ask him for a walk.

While he washed he remembered the funny touch of Lamech's hands on his arms and legs. It had felt like the leather in his workshop, and he was glad to wash it away.

When he went to bed his father came over. "Where have you been today, son?"

"Just walking around," he lied. He knew it was wrong, a wrong choice between good and bad to lie to his father, but he couldn't tell him he had walked up the hill with Lamech. "I was playing," he added.

"Tomorrow we'll clean the gun again. It's Saturday, we can do it in the evening. Would you like to help me?"

"Yes, Father. When shall we walk to the mountains?"

"Oh, next week I think. Gideon will come with us. You should go over to his farm sometime, he said he'd teach you to milk cows."

Nimrod wasn't sure whether to say good night to the sword on the wall, to the jeeps, or to the promised leather toy Lamech would give him.

His little body curled in bed and he hugged the white

pillow. He couldn't fall asleep immediately as he couldn't help thinking about the depths from which you couldn't climb if you made the wrong choice, and about the high tree he had climbed the other day and his fear that he could not climb down it, and about the guns they would clean tomorrow. And when at last he fell asleep he dreamed about Lamech, without his apron, climbing the tree in the white valley, and he heard him saying "I am strong," and the children laughing and shouting "Show us you're strong!" And when Lamech climbed the tree he fell down. Nimrod woke up, turned, and clung to the pillow, comforted by its warmth, and sank into deep sleep, with no dreams, no thoughts.

# 3

THEY started late in the afternoon. Nimrod carried a small bag, and Ivri and Gideon the rest of the things. They took some blankets and food, and intended to climb that night and descend the morning after.

In the bus, on the way to the Arab village on the southern slope, they didn't speak much. Nimrod was watching the road, and as the two men sat behind him he shared a seat with a woman who was carrying chickens and a goose in large baskets. She tried to talk to him. "What's your name, little boy?" He snubbed her and didn't answer.

"Where are you going?" This he would tell her, because it was something to be proud of. "To the mountain, to this one," he said pointing to the peak. "It's the highest in Israel."

"But you are so small, your father shouldn't let you climb."

"My father is taking me there. I'm not small. I'm very strong. I climbed the highest tree in Beit-On."

"You won't tell me your name?"

"No." And why should he? All these chickens, noisy and uncomfortable, and the silly ribbon with which she tied her hair back. Her hands were red, and her fat body shook as the bus struggled through the curves of the mountain road. When they left the bus the woman patted him on his head.

"Be strong, little man," she said.

He smiled at her then, for the first time, but only said "Sure," the way his father sometimes did.

Gideon was handsome and tall and strong. He had dark straight hair which he never combed, and his shirt revealed a hairy chest; he was said to have taken part in different operations. The villagers named him "the Rock," and said they wished their boys were like him. Nimrod didn't think he liked him. Gideon used to tease him, and he didn't like that at all.

"Will you faint on the way?" Gideon asked Nimrod. He didn't answer and pretended not to have heard. When Ivri was ahead of them, Gideon added: "If I had a son your age he'd be different. I think your father is too soft with you. And all these curls! Why don't you cut your hair very short?"

"Mother likes it that way."

"So you are Mother's boy, is that it? Would you like to run up the mountain?"

"No. I don't think so. Would you?"

"I'll show you!" And he started walking fast, passing Ivri and waving to them from above, mocking the little body which was struggling up the narrow path, trying to breathe properly, trying not to slip on stones and to choose the right place to put his sandaled feet.

The evening drew three silhouettes against the sky:

Gideon, large and hurrying, climbing as if taking a morning walk; Ivri, steady, wrapped in thought, his shorts too
long and his back slightly bent; and Nimrod, red-faced, not
caring to look around at the little village planted like a
toy below, or the forest to the right, or the many little
flowers around, his eyes fixed on the next few feet of the
road, his hands hanging like two superfluous objects, and
his legs, strained and heavy, making each step carefully
and without assurance.

He lost sight of Gideon and Ivri, and after climbing
higher he reached a patch of ground where they were both
sprawled on their backs, feet high, water bottles open. And
they were joking. He was really angry. They greeted him.
Gideon's white teeth—unlike Lamech's—showed when he
said, "Hello mountain man! Well done, fellow. But you're
so red! Shall we leave you here and go on? We can pick
you up on our way down. Or do you still feel like climbing up?"

Nimrod didn't speak. He looked at his father, who
smiled and said, "Leave the boy alone, he's very good!
Strong, isn't he?"

The boy continued. He didn't want to lie down, feeling
he'd never be able to get up again. He dared not look all
the way up to the peak, so, eyes on the ground, he went on.
Alone. Hearing the men behind laughing, "Little hero!
Won't you rest? Little hero!" And it was his father who
said it, he knew his father loved him very much, but he
cried to be loved not as a little hero. He was thirsty, and
had stopped for a drink of water from the bottle he carried
when Gideon's figure appeared. "So, you're thirsty too.
Only you prefer to be alone. One of these lonely boys,
aren't you. Maybe you'd prefer *us* to stay behind."

Nimrod recorked the bottle and went on. Reaching a rock where he had to use his hands he saw Gideon's hand stretched toward him to help, and he took it, as he knew he had to, and his little hand felt lonely and neglected in Gideon's hand. It was like grasping firm wood. The hand was dry and rough and hard, and there was nothing warm about it. He smiled his thanks and went on.

In a way Nimrod envied Gideon. Not that he cared to be like him, but there was something massive about this man; he seemed not to have to think, he seemed to be a permanent continuous proof of physical potency, he was a part of the view and the scenery, and all was so easy for him, so simple, his routine answer to most questions was —No problems! While for Nimrod everything was a problem. Why should he climb the mountain, and why didn't his father speak, and would he be less tired going down, and where did the flowers get their color from, where was the woman in the bus going, and what was Mother doing alone now?

And in no time at all they reached the peak. It was unexpected, as Nimrod had lost all sense of time or distance; there was only the pain between his ribs, and his mind working, and he was singing something to himself when he heard Gideon singing loudly, and he didn't feel the weight of the bag any more and there it was, the end of the effort, and Ivri and Gideon watching him make the last few steps, and Ivri saying to Gideon: "I told you he'd do it, he's my son! Bless you, Nimrod, Father is proud of you. Now take your bag off and put your legs up and rest. And look! So many flowers!"

Gideon laughed! "Flowers! Look at the view! Look at the valley below. Look at Safad above the rocks. Look at the stones, the strength of the mountain, look down and be proud of the way you did this, little boy. Flowers you can get in the forest of Beit-On."

Still they are so pretty, thought Nimrod, and lay down.

He felt sick for a moment, the blood running to his head from the legs and staying there. He shut his eyes and could hear hammers nailing his forehead to the soil, he saw spots, funny ones, red and blue and fast changing, and when he opened his eyes he felt like shutting them again and never, but never, getting up or moving.

His father collected wood for a fire and Gideon lit it. It was dark by now and Nimrod was still lying in the same spot. Then he heard his father approaching and sitting down next to him. "You are not tired, are you?" he asked. He had this manner of asking questions which included the answer he expected.

Nimrod smiled and stood up. He washed his hands and face with water, and joined the men near the fire.

There was something odd in the atmosphere, a kind of worship of nature, and the fire, and the Turkish coffee boiling. Gideon had put on an Arab headdress and now he began to sing loudly with Ivri joining him. And the fire seemed to whisper with them, the mountain was friendly, and the night cool but bright. Ivri was happy. He kept thinking about his village in Russia. When he was Nimrod's age he couldn't climb mountains, he was weak and white and soft, and afraid of his body and of nature. And here it was all free. He wanted to sing an ode to the rocks and the narrow paths and to his son. He clapped with the rhythm of Gideon's song, and Nimrod joined him, the lights of Safad winked at them from a distance, and the coffee poured warmth into their limbs. He thought he could dance only he was ashamed to, for this was a man's occasion. The three of them felt the masculine in them, in the effort, in the achievement, in being tired, in relaxing, and for Ivri it was more than that, it was his son next to him, a man, a Hebrew man.

The song climbed the tree-lined road into the cloudless skies, and rested on the grass and rocks, and was echoed back from the cliffs, and Nimrod was strangely happy. He wasn't envious of Gideon any more, he was one of them. He wanted to hear it said, shouted. "Did I faint, Gideon?"

"No, young man. You did it, damn it, you're as strong as a rock. Be careful or I'll get jealous. They'll start calling you the 'Rock' in the village, you curly-headed slip of a boy. Shake hands?"

They shook hands, almost a ritual ceremonious shake and Ivri wanted to kiss his son, but he didn't. He shook his little hand and wondered if Miriam would be as proud as he was.

Nimrod unfolded a blanket, wrapped himself, and lay on his back counting the stars. He felt at home up on the mountain, and wasn't sleepy, only tired.

"Father, a story tonight?"

"Yes, son." Ivri took his blanket and lay next to him. He told a story and yet he was actually talking to himself, or to his father, or to the policeman he had feared in his village. He told him the stories of heroes, many heroes, he spoke about men without fears, he spoke of free people, of the land. There was heart in his voice, almost tenderness at moments, and then sadness again and vigor. He didn't notice Nimrod's falling asleep, and continued to tell stories into the night. Gideon was snoring in restless sleep behind the large tree, and Ivri was worshiping the stars, his hands playing with grains of hard soil. And when he turned to watch his son he saw he was asleep. Feeling almost guilty he bent over him to kiss him. The little head moved, the eyes opened and shut, and he sank back again into peaceful sleep.

Who is strong—who is strong—who is strong—was in the wind, like a stream of water rolling little stones down the valley—

I am strong—strong—strong—echoed back voices, and the charm of nature, and Ivri's voice, and Gideon's teasing smile demanded—show us you're strong—strong—strong—

And little men in suits like those in town were climbing the mountain and disappearing, and hero Nimrod was walking forward and helping them and smiling from the peak, and yelling into the empty valley—I am strong, his voice joining the sound of bells tied to the goats' necks, joining Ivri's voice telling stories, always the same stories, joining Lamech's toothless smile dancing among the tombstones, and sinking back into dreamless sleep.

They woke with dawn to watch the pink-and-orange sun rising. It turned into a white blaze as they went down toward Safad, almost running.

# 4

I̲T WAS a hot Saturday and Nimrod didn't feel like going all the way down to the lake. He knew that Lamech went to the synagogue on Saturdays and he decided he'd go with him.

He wasn't sure, but thought he should put on a shirt, which he did, and left the house as if sneaking toward unknown adventure.

Lamech was having his tea when he arrived there, and when Nimrod came in and saw him he knew definitely that he wanted to go to the synagogue very much. Maybe this would explain to him the difference between Lamech and his father, or Lamech and Gideon.

"I'm going with you to the pink house!"—for some reason the synagogue was painted light pink—"Will you take me?"

"Yes, little one, but does your father know?" He looked at Nimrod, who didn't answer. "I see. All right, you may still come."

He picked out a large handkerchief and tied its ends into little knots and fitted it on the boy's head.

"What's that for?" giggled Nimrod.

"Just a rule. You have to cover your head when you go into the house of God." Lamech had a little cap he stuck on his head, and folding Nimrod's improvised hat they left the cottage.

The next two hours were unreal, he couldn't at all connect it with Beit-On. The few old men moving rhythmically when praying, their lips repeating unheard words, their faces remote and their eyes shut—and Nimrod among them. He saw the cupboard where they kept the Holy Scriptures, and they all had the book of prayers in their hands. He could read in it, but only slowly, and some of the words he didn't understand, it wasn't at all like any of the books in school. He wasn't sure about what he was to do, and he had tears in his eyes when one of the old men pushed him and said, "Pray, child." Not really wanting to he let his little body move forward and back with the sound of quiet voices. He tried to shut his eyes but he lost his balance. And it was hot. Never on a hot day did he wear a shirt, and the funny cap on his head added to his discomfort. He watched Lamech, and he wasn't like the rest of them. He wasn't moving, his eyes were almost open, and he had a smile on his face. Not that he smiled with his lips. Rather it was an inner light, or maybe the face looked less wrinkled, but he was content and relaxed.

Nimrod was holding the old little book and trying to understand the meaning. He was thinking, too, that maybe he should have gone to the lake, and what would his father say if he saw him there, and he was reciting the stories Lamech told him, stories of David and Moses and other heroes, and he wondered if they used to look like this and stand and pray every Saturday. He imagined his tall slim father as a little boy in a suit, reading fast from the book, and praying in a place where it was snowy, and the children of the village mocked him when he went out.

He knew the children of Beit-On would too. It wasn't the kind of thing you would do when playing "Who is strong?" and somehow he couldn't think about the chairs and books and stools and the cupboard covered with a velvet curtain as a challenge. They wouldn't shout like the lake and the hills: Show us you are strong. Maybe they would say as Lamech did—love! But no—not even that. They seemed dumb to him, not mysterious any more, just objects, unbelonging, fascinating in their age and meaningless to him. But he knew they weren't really different, and he was enchanted by the expression of content mixed with endless suffering on their faces. His father was either happy, or angry, but you could never see Ivri's inner self projected in beauty to his face. So he watched the faces and now there was light on his own face, he knew he could love, as Lamech wanted him to, and he also knew he could be strong, and he wasn't afraid, and he felt the strength within him and musingly moved as if praying. And then he felt Lamech's hand touching his asking him to follow.

When they went out of the pink house they met Gideon. He stopped, surprised. He looked at them both, and then shouted angrily: "You little bastard! What were you doing in there? Making fun of old people? Is this a new trick? All the boys are down in the lake and you"—Gideon noticed the funny cap Nimrod was wearing—"what's that?"

"A hat. You can't pray without a hat."

"You—praying? Wait till Ivri hears your story. You

could have done something productive on Saturday morning, like feeding the cattle. Come, say shalom to Lamech,
and then you're coming with me."

"I'm not. And I don't mind if you tell my father. I went
to see. It's part of Beit-On too, isn't it?"

"Yes. Only it isn't your department." Gideon held Nimrod's collar and pulled him. "We're going home," he said.

Lamech carefully folded the little cap, without untying
the knots, and put it in his pocket. He approached Nimrod,
put his hand on his shoulder. "It's all right, boy, go home.
And you can come with me some other day. We'll make
the birthday toy this week. Now go home and rest. It's
all right."

"Toys! Synagogue! A nice farmer you make, Nimrod.
Go home!"

He didn't go home. He knew Gideon was going there to
talk to Ivri. But he went up the hill to the secret meeting
place. Two girls were picking flowers there. He passed
near them and one of them—with serious eyes and long
plaited hair—asked him, "You want some red flowers?"

"No, Rina. And what are you doing here anyway? It's the
boys' place."

"The flowers aren't yours, are they? You want to play?"

"No. I'm cross."

"I didn't do anything." Rina and her friend sat on a
rock arranging the flowers. Nimrod didn't really feel like
being alone, and he joined them.

"You're not afraid here? You know there are big men
under these stones."

"They aren't big. They are just dead."

"You'll be put under a stone like this one day." Nimrod
wanted to scare them. It would make it easier to face Ivri
later.

"I don't mind. I'll be a grandmother when they put me under a stone."

"And the worms will eat you, and then you'll be in hell."

The younger girl had tears in her eyes. "I don't want to be under a stone."

"See what you did?" Rina said. "Now tell her something else."

"I've been to the pink house with Lamech!"

The two girls bent forward excited. "Tell us! What do they do in there?"

Nimrod felt old and clever. He got up and imitated the old men in prayer.

"Did you laugh? It looks funny."

"No. I prayed."

The girls didn't seem to believe him, but they left it at that.

"I also climbed the tree in the white valley, and the Azmon, the highest mountain above Safad." He was vaunting his achievements proudly. It was an attentive, appreciative audience.

"Show us your muscles!"

He flexed his arm muscles, and let the girls touch them. They said, "Oh!" and tried their own.

"Were you afraid to climb the tree?"

"I'm never afraid. I liked it."

"You're not afraid to go out in the dark?"

"Never, ask my father."

He thought about it though. He knew he should never be afraid. And he wondered about it too. He thought it would be good never to be afraid. He left the girls with their flowers. He agreed to take one flower from each. He threw them away just before entering his house.

Miriam was alone in the house. Ivri and Gideon's voices could be heard from the orange grove.

"Nimi! Why did you go to the synagogue?"

"Why not, Mother?" He became angry. "You tell me things to do like climbing the mountain, and going places, and when I do something which is not important you're angry. Why not? It's in the village. People from the village go there. I didn't do anything bad."

"No, it's only strange. We never go there, we don't think one needs to. And all of a sudden, of all boys in the village, it's our son who comes out of the pink house. It's just strange, not bad. Your father will explain it to you better."

"So he will," said Ivri. "You're too young to know what's best. That's why you've got parents who can tell you. Now listen, boy, Lamech isn't the friend for you, and the pink house isn't a game. Years ago it was necessary for us to obey regulations and keep our religion. Now we have land instead.

"You are an Israeli. I was only a Jew. You know what my name was in Russia? Motl, can you imagine that? Motl, and I changed it to Ivri. I left my clothes behind and some of my family, and found a new God. He is in the orange blossom, in the feeling of the soil. Don't you feel it, boy?" He picked up some earth and poured it into the boy's palm. "Grasp it, feel it, taste it. There is your God. If you want to pray, boy, pray to the sky to bring rain to our land and not virtue to our souls. But you won't understand that.

"Don't go to Lamech. If you're bored, there is much work you can do. This week you can go with Gideon and learn to milk the cows. Your holiday is over soon, and you'll have your lessons. And one day when you're grown you'll see what I mean, and you'll appreciate what I tell you. Tell me you understand."

"I like the stories Lamech tells me. I wanted to know how the pink house looks inside, so I went. I'm hungry."

"Go wash and come to eat, Nimi," said Miriam. She didn't like this talk. She knew the boy wouldn't understand. Sometimes even she didn't. She came from the same background as Ivri and she was hurt when he told her there was no longer any need to light candles every Friday. But she accepted it, as she accepted all the changes in her life, and Ivri's idea that he should be the only one to take care of Nimrod's education. She went to the kitchen and put her motherly love into the cooking of her son's meal.

When, after lunch, Nimrod was left alone for a moment with Gideon, he looked at him and said proudly, "I will never come to you to milk the cows. I don't even care for your tractor. I don't think you are a rock at all."

"Come, come, boy. No need to be angry. I didn't tell Ivri about the toys and your talk with Lamech. And your being there wasn't a secret. Everybody saw you."

"Have you ever been inside?"

"No, why should I? I'm too busy for things like that. I know all about it."

"Well I wanted to know too."

"I'm going to the lake to join the boys, Mother! I'm going to the lake."

"Run boy, have fun, take care," she shouted as he ran out of the house. He thought it would be good to swim in cool water, not the deepest or lowest, just cool water. He would talk to the boys about school, and plan his birthday party, and he'd race with Udi and maybe beat him today. "Hey, Nimrod! Look what we found!" the boys shouted at him as he approached. It was an old automobile tire they had fished out of the water, and he joined their excitement.

# 5

UDI, then still the leader, got up to say there'd be no game the next day because of Nimrod's birthday. He would be nine, and the group was invited to the party.

Nimrod's mind was occupied with two things: what would be his father's gift, and whether Lamech would come and what secret toy he had for him. Ivri agreed that Lamech should be invited, as he was certain the old man wouldn't show up. But the old man did. The party was set up on the lawn behind the house. Early melons, late oranges, sweets—and a group of girls, their hair tied in ribbons and in white dresses, sitting in a circle watching the boys play games. Nimrod was playing when one of the girls exclaimed, "Look, look who's coming!" Twenty heads turned toward the path to see old Lamech approaching. And what a sight it was!

Lamech was wearing a white shirt! A white shirt that looked on him the way a black tail would look on a white mouse. His trousers looked pressed and his gray hair combed. He was holding two packages, one wrapped in brown paper and one stuffed in a leather bag. And Lamech was smiling.

Nimrod felt shy, almost embarrassed. Maybe he should have told the children that Lamech was coming, whispered it to them. Old Lamech, he should have said, comes because he's a friend, he knows so many stories!

Ivri, hearing the noise, came out. "Oh, it's you," he said. They shook hands, which Lamech found difficult to do with the packages, and the children surrounded them asking, "Show us! What did you bring!" Lamech joined the girls on the lawn and unpacked the brown package. Inside was a large box which he opened. It was full of sweets, chocolates cut in little squares, candies, and nuts. "That's for you, children."

The boys pushed each other, laughing, and Udi was the first one to take a candy. Then the others did too. Lamech had one of his toothless smiles on as he held the box looking at it being emptied. The kids weren't shy any more, they were grabbing the sweets and saying quick thank-yous.

Nimrod stood aside all this time. When the box was empty the boys went back to their game and the girls turned to watch, and Lamech's smile was still planted somewhere on his face and he seemed not to know what to do with the box. He reached it toward Nimrod. Nimrod approached, but there were no sweets left. So he took the box and put it aside and asked Lamech to sit down.

"No, come with me. I'll show you your gift." But one of the girls heard him and called out to the others:

"Lamech brought Nimrod a gift! He's going to show it!"

In a moment there was a circle of interested faces around the two, and Lamech, proud and happy, took the leather bag and pulled a rabbit out of it. A leather toy rabbit, large and funny and well stitched, sitting on its rear legs and looking at the world through two leather buttons placed as eyes, its ears long and soft. Rina grabbed it. "How pretty! We must name it! It's nicer than the toys in the shop! Did you make it, Lamech?" And then one of the boys started laughing, and the rest pointed at Nimrod. One whispered, "Nimrod the rabbit." They were passing the toy from hand to hand, and were commenting as they felt it, "Nimrod the rabbit!" "A toy for the baby!" "When I was three I had a toy like this one!" "He can fight the other boys with a rabbit now!" Lamech didn't hear. He was sure the children enjoyed his work and kept saying, "Thank you, little ones, thank you. Two whole nights, pieces of leftover leather, thank you children." And without asking Nimrod whether he did, he turned to him and said, "I'm glad you like it, I thought you would. I've got to go now." Nimrod took the rabbit and as he walked away with Lamech he heard Udi saying, "Nimrod will eat only carrots now, and will jump, and anyway he's probably as frightened as a rabbit!" The children shouted their agreement and went back to their game. And Nimrod held Lamech's hand and said to him, "It's the nicest toy rabbit ever made," and held it close to his white shirt, "and thanks for the sweets, the children were very happy." At this moment Ivri came out of the house. There was his son, his future Gideon, the one who climbed the mountain, who was so nice, standing with a toy rabbit and a silly old man.

"What's that?" He touched the toy with obvious disapproval.

"It's a gift from Lamech. Isn't it beautiful?"

"Yes. It's pretty. You're not going away, Lamech? Come in and have a glass of tea with me and Miriam. Here, Nimrod son, give me the rabbit. I'll put it in your room. You go play with the boys."

Reluctantly Nimrod obeyed and Lamech, as if obeying an order, stepped inside with Ivri.

"Have a chair, Lamech. Miriam! Some tea for Lamech!"

"Tell me now, I've wanted to talk with you for a long time. What do you want from my son?"

"Nothing, Ivri. I like the boy, we're friends, I tell him stories, he watches me at work. Nothing, Ivri."

"I don't like it, old man. You don't understand my little boy. He's good to you, he probably feels sorry for you, but that's all there is to it. And you don't want pity, do you? You haven't changed, Lamech, immigrating here hasn't really meant much to you. You don't care for the land, your skin isn't tanned, you're so, so—Jewish!"

"How dare you, Ivri! Motl, the son of Rabbi Pimchas, how dare you! Why do you think *you* are here? You think I love the land and the sun and the freedom any less than you do? I love it with my heart, not with my mind. Changing one's name doesn't change one's personality, and you are as frightened as Motl the son of Pimchas was. You have a lovely son, I care for him very much, but in God's name what are you doing to him?"

"None of your business. You know nothing about children. You wish he were like the Motls and Avramels of a Russian village. My boy is a new type."

"There is no new type in human beings, and your boy is a sensitive, kind human being. You take a piece of soft elastic leather, you beat it until it becomes as hard as iron, and then—anything will crack it! What do you get? You lose the leather, and you don't get iron."

"I want Nimrod to be brave."

"Being brave is good, but fearless is what you are making him. You cut a piece of him. You operate on him day and night, and do you know what he's afraid of? To be afraid—

this is the fear that masters him, until all others fears, human, normal, healthy ones, are pushed aside and stop existing. Your son will not be brave if you go on like this, he'll lose his ability to fear, and he'll hate you one day for it."

"Don't talk like this to me. After all I'm his father."

"Yes," pondered Lamech, "he'll hate you one day, and he'll love his toy rabbit, and it might be too late. He'll be too old for the rabbit and not old enough to be alone, like the leather and the iron."

"What's wrong with being fearless? Isn't that what we want our sons to be like?"

"One who cannot fear cannot love, and God wants us to love. Your son will want to love, and being fearless will mean being alone, so terribly alone, more alone than I am, or you."

"Me? Alone?"

"You try to change, you're not yourself, so you're alone. You're afraid of the people who know your old self, and you are not so sure about your new self, so you pour it into Nimrod. How selfish can a father get? You drive your son to jump into a deep pool just because you never had the chance or the will to jump into one. I'd better go. I speak too much."

"Yes, Lamech. You'd better go. The air of Israel or the village of Beit-On haven't made you any wiser. Shalom."

Ivri ignored Lamech's hand stretched out to shake his, and opened the door for him. Miriam came from the kitchen.

"But, Lamech, you're not leaving. The water has just boiled." She glanced at Ivri's hard face, and back at Lamech's.

"I have to go now. Some other time, Miriam. Thanks for

all. You've got a wonderful boy. Take care of him." He left.

"A toy rabbit. The old fool. Nimrod!"

Most of the boys had left and the remaining ones were opening the gifts and playing with the new games. The girls had all gone. Nimrod apologized to the remaining boys. "I have to go now. See you tomorrow." He ran into the house. "Yes, Father."

"Don't you want to see your gift?"

"Yes, Father, what is it? Show me!"

Ivri took a small parcel from his pocket, untied the string and paper, and there was a shabriah, an Arab pocket-knife, the kind to adjust to a belt and hang on your hip. It was in a brown leather sheath and had designs engraved on it. The handle was of wood, and the shining blade was clean and new. "Well! How do you like that! It's a real knife, you can cut everything with it!" Nimrod didn't know that he wanted to cut everything. He saw knives like this one hung on belts of older boys. They all wanted to have a shabriah, it was the dream of Udi and Moti and Yossi. And now he had one.

"It's a sharp one, Nimrod, you'll have to be careful. But it's a real one. When I was young I always wanted to have a shabriah that would cut everything. Never lose it. It's a grown-up's shabriah, and you can always use it. One day you'll have a son, and when he'll be nine you'll give it to him."

"Thank you, Father, it's a very nice one. Thank you."

Ivri thought proudly about it and joked, "It's so sharp you can even cut your toy rabbit's nails with it. It'll cut the hardest leather."

"Where is my rabbit?"

"In your room. You don't want to play with toys. Bedtime now, grown-up boy. With all those sweets you don't want any dinner, do you?"

"Not really, thank you, Father. Where is Mother?"

"Miriam! Nimrod likes our gift. He's not a child any more."

Miriam combed the boy's hair and sent him to bed.

He took the knife with him, and found the rabbit thrown in a corner. It looked funny because it was upside down. He took both gifts to bed with him. The bed was too small for both the rabbit and himself so he dragged up the chair and seated the toy opposite him. Next to it he put the knife. He didn't want to cut anything, and he smiled at the rabbit and touched its funny ear. The knife was very pretty, but he'd never want to cut anything with it.

He knew he could say "Good night, Rabbit," but he didn't know how to say good night to the knife. So he pulled the sheet over his face.

# 6

NIMROD knew a world war was on. Not much more than that. Some of the men of the village were gone, but Ivri remained. Gideon was gone, which didn't bother Nimrod much at the time, and listening to the news broadcast became an important part of their day; the grownups talked a lot about the war, but Nimrod didn't understand much of it, and since for him war had to do with tanks and jeeps, and he didn't see any, he continued being happy or worried about the same things. Ivri told him about the war. He used to try and explain it to the little boy. "You love this country?" "Sure." "You know, whatever happens, we won't leave it." "No." But this was natural, it had nothing to do with Ivri's stories or explanations. How could he think of leaving Beit-On, the lake and the highest tree, and the white valley and the secret meeting place?

The children of Beit-On played war games, but Nimrod knew it wasn't like this in real life, and as the winter approached he stayed indoors with his stamp collection and drawings, talked for long hours to the rabbit when his father was out, and helped much with the farm.

It was during this period that he quarreled with his parents. He felt an odd sensation of being guided, led, and dominated, and as he couldn't pin it down he was more disturbed. It was a combination of lack of attention for hours and days, and then, all of a sudden, as if to catch a ball of string rolling down a hill, they'd catch and pull, and roll back and pack and wrap and lay him on a shelf to rest. He started having fears. First he thought he wasn't their child, and then he thought, and was sure, that his mother didn't really love him, and he grew jealous of his father. He tried to be bad and naughty, and his father liked it. For Ivri it was a sign of independence and maturity, his boy turning into an impudent proud man, and he thought it good for him. Miriam was worried because of the war, and Ivri forbade her to let Nimrod become aware of her emotions. So she kept away from him.

As he was ten already, and grown up, Miriam stopped kissing him when he went to bed, and Ivri didn't tell him bedtime stories. Lamech was still an escape, but even the old man was concerned with the war and his stories changed too. He kept telling the boy about a free state, and possible war with the Arabs—a term used often then, although the only Arab Nimrod knew was an old woman, Naifa, who came with a donkey to sell vegetables or watermelons every week. She was dressed in black and he couldn't talk to her, but the watermelons were red and juicy and he couldn't see why they should fight Naifa, or what would happen to her if they did.

So he kept to himself.

Twice he tried to find love. Once he pretended to be

sick. He said his head ached and he felt weak and sick.
He wouldn't move from bed.

"You'll be all right, son," Ivri said. "It's just weakness."

"Rest a day in bed, it's always good for you," said Miriam.
And that was all. They knew he wasn't really ill. He got
dressed and left the house. It was a cold day and he went
to the lake. Now he wanted to be sick, very sick. He'd swim
in the cold water, maybe he'd even drown, and he'd come
back and be taken to a hospital. Miriam would have to be
near him all the time, and Ivri would be worried, not because of the war or the rain, but because of him, Nimrod.

The water was cooler than he thought, and he tried to
put his foot in but dared not and came back.

"I almost drowned today," he lied. "I was at the lake
and almost drowned."

"How's that?" Ivri asked, doubting.

"Just as I told you," he said.

He tried to attract attention; he was difficult, rebellious,
and hard. He started lying, and then he did a second
thing which was disturbing. He stole money. Money in
Beit-On wasn't something the children were concerned
with. They'd get their few piasters every week and spend
it in the stores, buying sweets or ice cream from the man
who came every week. So Miriam kept money in a drawer
and Nimrod took a note—a one-pound note. He never
had had that much money, and when he took it his heart
was almost leaping out of his body. He was sweating and
nervous, but he took it and put it in his pocket.

Nimrod was stealing attention, he was stealing back
his bedtime stories and good-night kiss.

He took the pound and ran quickly to the secret meeting
place. It was empty, and he dug a hole in the ground and

put the money in it. He had no need for it, he hid it safe and warm, as if securing the love he had lost, and he went back home.

They never noticed it. Both Ivri and Miriam thought it was the other who had taken it, and Nimrod was annoyed and disappointed. First he tried to oppose Ivri in what he said or suggested. He'd pretend to be weak and soft and quiet when he knew Ivri wanted him to be strong and brave. But when that didn't work, he decided on the opposite.

He'd be stronger, he'd be the strongest. He'd be all his father wanted him to be, and more so. Nimrod, aged ten, decided he'd outdo Gideon. He'd climb higher trees, and he realized then there were higher trees than the one in the white valley. He'd be braver, the bravest, and he thought then that actually he was not afraid of anything. He wanted his parents to fear him, and be afraid for him. He might even climb the white mountain on the other side of the lake. He didn't need his parents as they didn't seem to need him, and he'd prove it.

All of a sudden, he hated the toy rabbit, and he took his shabriah knife and stuck it into his belt. He was strong! He'd show them he was strong! All of them!

Lamech was very sad when he saw Nimrod doing what he was doing. He knew Ivri's plan was succeeding, he knew the boy was losing his fears, partly because he was being taught to, and partly because he wanted to prove he was strong and gain attention.

"You've changed, little one," he told him.

"I'm not a little one any more; I milk the cows already."

"You're so confused, but it's not your fault though. But you shouldn't yield to it. Come, let's see what the leather bits look like today."

"Like nothing. I can cut the hardest leather bits with my knife. I can even cut the rabbit with my knife."

Lamech was irritated. "You don't like the rabbit any more?"

"I'm not a baby. Do you want it back? You can give it to some baby girl."

"No, Nimrod. I don't want it back."

"I'm going now, Lamech."

"When will you come again?"

"I don't know. Shalom."

When the boy left, Lamech took off his apron, as he could think better without it, made himself a glass of tea, with lots of sugar this time, and sat thinking about the boy. It couldn't be true, because he knew Nimrod better. Why would he behave like this? It was either Ivri's success, or as he thought more likely—failure, or revenge on someone. But who?

He didn't believe very much in the New Jew. He knew they should love the soil, the lake, the mountains. He knew they should be free, and ageless and daring. He knew a war would come and they would have to fight. But Nimrod frightened him. The quality of his eyes had changed, it was like looking at empty wells, where you couldn't see your own image, where it was dark and meaningless. He knew Nimrod had started descending the ladder, and he was only a boy of ten. He could see the gap between the boy and himself and his father. He could see it growing and he feared it.

It wasn't human, there was something of a little monster in the way Nimrod said he could cut the rabbit.

The destructive in the Jew, he thought, the self-pity, the heroism at moments—bordering almost on the ridiculous—is changed into the self-destructive, which is encouraged and glorified. He tried, while sipping his tea, to think it was his imagination. Nimrod wouldn't change, and anyway he was too young to know what was better. He did love the rabbit and he wouldn't cut it, and he was now just a moody little boy.

Though it was early Lamech felt very tired, and as he had taken his apron off earlier he thought he could afford a short nap. So on the chair, his legs on a stool, he shut his eyes, and fell into a light sleep.

When he woke up an hour later, in the dark, he couldn't remember much of the dream, only that Nimrod was cutting the rabbit into pieces, and placing them with a smile in a row, and next to them Nimrod placed flowers, red and blue, the flowers he liked so much, and then, moving, not really meaning to, he upset the vase, the flowers were scattered on the floor, and the boy cried, wept, and it was Lamech, he himself, who was laughing in mockery, loud laughter watching the boy trying to collect the flowers, which were perishing, and then trying to stick the cut rabbit together, and as Lamech was laughing the rabbit when put together jumped out through the window, and the boy was left with the dead flowers and tears, and when Lamech tried to stop laughing and approached him, the boy pushed him away, down, down, down—

He tasted the tea in the dark. It was cold and stale.

Silly old man, he said to himself, you're jealous of Ivri, you'd want to have a son like Nimrod. You're no good, cutting leather, working on shoes which will wear out, and when you die not a shoe will be left, and not a son to weep for you. "He was a funny type," they would say in the village.

Lamech fixed the light in the oil lamp and picked up a small mirror. He couldn't remember when he last had looked at himself in a mirror.

"Better face it, silly old type."

He stared at his own eyes, and it made him feel good for they weren't like empty wells. Something looked back at you, and he wondered when Nimrod would come back, and whether he would come back at all.

## 7

THE war started and ended, and to the children in the Galilee village of Beit-On it didn't mean much. Some of the men were away, some were training for what they called "our light," but as no tanks or jeeps appeared in the valley of Beit-On the children carried on with their activities. Gideon was not back yet, and a rumor spread that he was wounded and would be put in a hospital in Jaffa. As it was holiday time, Nimrod was sent to Haifa to visit an aunt.

Before he left, Ivri, who didn't talk to him often these days, considering the period as "difficult" in the boy's life, said to him, "Remember when you're in the city that you are a Beit-On boy. We want to be proud of you. Children in town are more spoiled, they aren't used to work, so don't learn from them but teach them."

While he was packing Nimrod wondered whether town children had little knives like his, which he was taking with him.

He would teach them, of course he would. They didn't play real games, they probably played with toys. His father

said they didn't work, so he would certainly be the strongest, maybe even a leader. And he was. Being independent
and bright he learned how to get around alone in a few
days, he knew the streets around his house, and soon he did
have a group, with himself, Nimrod of Beit-On, as the
leader.

Actually it was rather easy, as the children of the neigh-
borhood were on vacation and didn't have much to do.
And as Nimrod looked strong and brown, and maybe a
year older than most of them, they accepted it.

Nimrod told them stories, not Lamech's, but his father's,
and he also invented some. He told them the story of climbing the mountain, and after that none doubted his ability
to be the leader. And he decided to teach them the secret
game of "Who is strong?"

He took the children to a courtyard, where cats and
garbage-pickers were the only frequenters. He thought it
would be fun to make them swear an oath, like an Indian
vow he had read about.

The frightened group of children watched him with
admiration. He drew a circle in the sand and told them to
stand around it. He made each of them leap into the circle,
and while doing so say "whatever is said and done in this
group is not to be told to strangers. I promise to keep it
all secret and will accept punishment if I fail to do so."

They didn't really understand what they were in for.
They thought it fun and wondered what the leader meant
by punishment. Nimrod was very serious, imitating Udi
and thinking of what tasks town children could choose
when they played the game. He thought about his father
whom he hadn't felt like talking to recently. He knew he'd
be proud of him. Hadn't he told him to teach them? And
what else could he teach them?

They obeyed his orders to sit, and after explaining the game he stood up.

"Who is strong?" he asked with assurance. It wasn't as impressive here, as the secret meeting place wasn't half as good as the Beit-On one, and instead of an echo from the mountains, you got the noise of vehicles from Haifa's main street.

A thin boy stood up immediately. "I'm strong," he said in a matter-of-fact voice.

The children failed to remember what to do next.

But it's their first time, Nimrod thought, forgiving, and re-explained.

The boy chose to climb a fence, and jump from it, standing.

"All right," Nimrod said, "but it isn't really much proof. You'd better think of something real hard next."

They tried to, and some did. They grew to like the strange game, their sense of competition was developed, and they thought how clever the boy from the village was. And they admired his pocketknife, as all they had as knives could never cut a toy rabbit.

When they did the second round, Nimrod teased the first thin boy, Abraham, whom they called Avi.

"Well, this time you won't get away with a low fence. Better choose something difficult if you want to remain in the group."

Avi, whose parents were rich, and who was a spoiled little boy, did indeed want to remain in the group, so he said, "I'll cross the main road just before a car comes."

"All right," Nimrod said. He thought it to be a real task. They went to the main road. Nimrod had no fear of machines as he didn't know any. The tractors were slow and friendly, and the village truck and bus came and went once a day only.

As it was the end of the day, he was slightly bored with the children, and wanted to get it over with fast.

"Go ahead, Avi, or are you really strong?" The other kids were silent. They didn't like the idea. Some left, and the rest strolled down the pavement. Nimrod was left alone with Avi.

"Go ahead, cross. What are you waiting for? I'm hungry."

Avi did. There was a noise, and then voices, many voices. Nimrod looked at the scene. He couldn't see much as there were people around a small van that had come to a stop in the middle of the street, and as he approached he saw Avi lying flat, crying in pain, his leg bleeding.

"It's his fault," he cried, when he saw Nimrod. "It's his game. I didn't want to do it!"

Nimrod didn't really care much, and the blood irritated him, but this was the game. He was annoyed with Avi for telling the people, after the secret vow he had sworn, and, hands in pockets, he strolled away from the scene.

It was difficult to say whether Nimrod's indifference was due to extreme horror and a feeling of guilt, or to the complete lack of it, as the game and its tasks were natural things to him. Avi's breaking his leg didn't seem to him tragic. He thought when he went back to Beit-On perhaps Avi could be the leader of the group. It didn't occur to him the children wouldn't want to go on playing the game.

That evening was very unpleasant. The parents of the children came to his aunt to complain. He sat aloof and remote, munching his supper, listening with joy to the accusing voices.

"Great thing indeed! Fine game! Our new generation of farmers, that's what they teach their sons to do."

"He could have killed Avi, pushing him like this, did you tell him?"

"Yes. He could have killed him! And I thought of sending my boy to the village, but with games like this . . ."

"And my boy told me Nimrod carries a knife! Is that the idyllic village life we're preaching?"

"Where is the boy?"

Nimrod swallowed the last bit of bread and stepped into the room.

"I am here. It's not my aunt's fault. It's a game we play all the time. So he broke his leg, so what? I did once too. It's fun to have a plaster cast, you can write things on it."

"Do you realize you could have killed him?"

"Stop it!" his aunt said, and held him next to her. "He's a boy, he was naughty, but they were playing. It was Avi's idea to cross the street like that."

"He didn't die, did he?" asked Nimrod.

"Little monster! How dare you talk like that! Do you know what you're saying?" The women were angry and nervous. Each of them imagined Nimrod pushing her own son into disaster. The "little monster" was bored with the scene. He rather knew he had done something wrong, but he wasn't sure which of the things he had done was wrong. He missed Beit-On, all seemed to be so simple and direct there. Even Lamech was simpler than these women. So he said he would go back home. He left for his bedroom, and planned to leave the next morning. He'd tell his father and the boys all about it.

"What a strange little thing!" he heard them saying. "Nothing childish about this one! He's so serious and cruel!"

"I bet his mother never kisses him good night!" He felt tears coming, but he put on his pajamas and slipped into bed. So what? He's not a baby, he doesn't want to be kissed good night. He felt like saying bad words, like cursing, but he couldn't think of any words, and as the voices couldn't be heard any more he relaxed.

Ivri didn't say much. He didn't notice how Miriam shed a tear and stroked the toy rabbit. He didn't notice how Nimrod cleaned his knife, and he preferred not to think about it.

He didn't like the story. He preferred to think it was a reaction to Lamech's stories and wished Gideon was there. He took Nimrod to milk the cows with him.

"Don't worry, son. You'll be all right."

"I am."

Odd, Ivri thought, the boy doesn't talk much lately, he doesn't laugh with joy, he's rather obedient and withdrawn. He attributed it to growing up, and waved the thoughts away. There was enough trouble aside from this—the end of one war and prospects of another, a drought last summer, Gideon wounded, and one of the cows sick.

When Nimrod told Lamech the story, the old man grew very sad, and continued cutting leather. He didn't wish to comment. It was all wrong, it was his failure, and it was all very wrong and dangerous. He wished he could take the boy away with him for a while, somewhere where he needn't prove anything, where people found it necessary to grow kind and soft and not courageous and tough.

He'd dance with him and sing and tell him stories, funny ones, and make the boy laugh. It had been a long time since he saw him laugh. And he'd make him do good things, and they'd play like two children. But there they were, in Beit-On between wars, after a drought, a Beit-On of people who had immigrated with the decision to do things differently, better. Beautiful Beit-On, like a pearl planted in the mountains, with the view of the lake and the white cap on the peak of Mt. Chermon. A Beit-On of people who changed from Motl into Ivri and named their sons Nimrod—the hunter, the brave—bow and arrow instead of toy arrows and rabbits. He knew he'd repeat himself if he said all these things aloud, once again, so he looked sadly at the boy. "You're a good boy, Nimrod. You'll forget about Avi and anyway you don't like the town. I'll tell you a story."

Nimrod felt like hearing one. He smiled, he felt so tired and weak and lost, and he came closer and sat on the floor, putting his head in Lamech's lap, staring at nothing. "Yes, tell me a story."

Lamech told him a fairy tale, with dwarfs and princes and houses made of cakes, and he was playing with the moon, throwing it to the princess who laughed back at him, and he was riding on the clouds and in white carts, and he was eating candies from a plate made of sunlight, and the leather bits on the floor grew into shapes and he picked them up and laughed when they were funny. He was so very tired, as only a little boy can be after pushing another little boy into the street when a car was passing. He was so tired that Lamech had to help him stand up and send him back home.

## 8

NIMROD was thirteen, and it was a strange year. It was strange when Gideon was brought home, and they wouldn't let Nimrod visit him. Not for some time, Ivri said. It was strange because Nimrod started feeling the existence of his body; and he was the leader now.

His curls almost disappeared, and instead of girlish names, the children called him "Little Rock," and then "Rocky." It was again a bad year for the crops, and the people of Beit-On were walking with their heads turned sadly toward the sky.

"They don't pray," said Lamech, "and rain won't come." True they didn't pray, and the bright sun pouring its white intoxicated light across the valley was merciless, drying the seeds and the water wells, turning the green into yellow, into gray, and into nothing.

All solids seemed to melt this year, and the rhythm of life to slow, and it was strange because inside Nimrod's body and mind things happened, and grew from yellow to green, into blossom. And with the tranquillity of the

village, the eyes searching for clouds, and Gideon's locked
house, there was life inside him, curious, permanently sur-
prising, puzzling. And as there was no boy to share it with,
this which was both pleasant and frightening, there was
loneliness. And he was the leader, the little rock. His body
was nonexistent before. Now it was an instrument. When
he played with it, Miriam stopped him and Ivri said he'd
spank him if he touched his organs. So he did it at night,
in fear.

His parents' bodies were covered always. There was
curiosity, and fear. Little girls' bodies were something the
boys talked about, and when he was ten he had made a deal
with Rina, he had shown her his, and so had she. He had
found it funny and curious, but knew he was not to tell
anybody. They had made a vow and a promise about it,
and he kept it.

But now he had to ask Udi, who was older, and Udi told
him all about it. They went to Cemetery Hill, and Udi told
him about the birth of children, and what happened to
him when he started feeling his body. Udi told him what to
do, and how he would feel later, and he felt content. He
understood. It was his secret, but he knew about it.

And one day they let him visit Gideon. The house,
usually with all its doors and windows opened, was shut,
the curtains drawn, and in an armchair was Gideon, or
what was left of him.

One hand, one leg, head in bandages—and it was more
than a year since it had happened—the smell of medicines,
silence. And Nimrod didn't feel anything. Either he didn't
sense the cruelty and magic, or he did and accepted it, but
he didn't feel anything. He wasn't sorry, or surprised, or
shocked. It only emphasized his own body, whole and alive,
but he wanted to know how it had happened. It was a mine,

but Gideon wouldn't tell details. "It was just a mine," he said, "and it was muddy and dirty and ugly, and I was a fool," he said.

"Were you scared?"

Gideon hesitated. "That's why it happened. I did not think. I just went, and stepped on it, and my silly stupid coward friends who wouldn't go, they can walk now, they can hold a girl with both arms. I didn't think, or feel, not a thing. See Nimi"—how long since anyone had called him Nimi—"I don't feel when it's like that, it makes me sick to think about myself like that. See Nimi, the ones who were scared can walk. And what will be now? What will be?" He saw that the bandage below the eyes was wet, he knew the man was crying, the rock was shedding tears, and he, the leader, the little rock, he didn't care very much. A pity, he thought, I like Gideon. But we can't walk to the white mountain together. He knew what he meant when he said he didn't think, he knew it well, and was proud. Lamech would feel and think, Ivri might, but he thought he wouldn't. He knew now that if he'd be sent somewhere, far away, he'd just go. And if he'd be told—jump, he'd jump. He felt he was able to separate the activity from the emotion. Pray, Lamech said. Praying won't help Gideon. Maybe Ivri was right, it's the new type, the rocks.

"Would you like me to come often?"

"Yes, Nimi. Here, come closer. Sit on the bed, let me hold your hands. Yes, both, my hand is large enough for that." He sighed as if in pain.

"Does it hurt?"

"It hurts. Shall I tell you my dream last night? Please let me talk, and talk to me, I don't feel the pain when I talk."

"Tell me your dream."

"I stepped out of my body, and I could do everything. I was light and bright, and I walked fast with a girl, and I held her in both hands, but, it wasn't my hands, I mean, my body wasn't there at all. I hugged her with my heart and kissed her with my feelings and walked on my mind and thoughts, and behind me I could hear the sound of crutches and see an invalid body following me. It was too slow to reach me but it pulled me back, and the girl went on and on, and I was dragged back, to wake up in pain, inside this mask.

"I'll go out of my mind. I lie for hours thinking what will happen. I wasn't afraid for a moment when I had my body ready to operate, muscles ready to answer, limbs ready to act. Now that I've lost it, I'm afraid. And what is left?"

"Oh, you can read, and talk, and your mind works," answered Nimrod seriously.

"Not for long. Rocks have no minds. Nimi, what will you do in life?"

"Work. Be on the farm. We'll have a war, Father says. I'll fight, I'll just continue." He laughed. "I'll have sons, maybe many sons."

When Nimrod left the house, he preferred not to think about it. Lately he had found out he could control his thoughts, and he needn't think about things which he preferred to push back somewhere. Ivri tried to talk to him about what he called "the situation," and the boy was fascinated. At the beginning, just to annoy Ivri, he would say he was not interested, but he was. He started knowing where he was, and not taking it for granted. He also knew there would be a war. He knew now why he should be strong, and what for. He felt his mind getting more and more involved, and his body and his emotions he put aside. As he couldn't really hate his enemy, Ivri would tell him,

"You're to trust nobody, there are no real friends, you should never expect anything of people." He would touch his muscles and say, "That's your only friend. Strength. You are a man. You don't need friends. Beware of kindness, tenderness, warmth. In most cases they lead to disaster. If people fear you, they respect you, if not, they'll overpower you and you'll be left to their mercy. If you ever need anything, come to me, or," he added reluctantly, "to your mother. See, son, we can't afford weak ones and cowards. If they are old, like silly Lamech, let them die in peace. But the young ones—rocks we need."

"And Gideon? He is a weak one now."

"Useless, poor thing. But he did his share, in the wrong war too, and he can't think straight now, something is wrong with him, he doesn't know how to take it."

"What will happen if I'm wounded in a war, Father?"

"You won't be wounded in a war. It's the weak ones who get hurt, the ones who are not sure, and they stay in one place. You're sure and clever and brave. You needn't think of it."

"No."

Though he was thirteen he still placed his rabbit in his room, on the shelf; his other toys he gave away, but this one he wouldn't; the group of boys met less often as they all were working on the farms after school, and formed smaller groups of two or three boys. They started cursing, wearing blue shirts, and paying attention to their looks. They talked to the girls.

The boys of Beit-On never spent much time at home, as it was school early, and then work on the farm, and then meeting and walking along in pairs, discussing the lack of rain and "the situation" while eating nuts. In school they wrote essays on subjects like—What's Demanded of Us!—

The Place of a Youngster in New Israel—Is a War a Solution? They had no chance to mature from children into adolescents, into men. There was no time; too much to be done, too much to lose in a long process, too heavy a responsibility.

So they combed their hair the way grownups do, and examined each others' muscles, and looked to the sky for rain, and used expressions their fathers used, and prepared themselves for vague unknown tasks.

If war hadn't been in the air, it would have been necessary to invent it. Ivri's generation fought the land and conquered it. They took the first step of the change. Gideon's generation fought a world war. And both injected their spirit and strength into Nimrod's in a large national manner. It wasn't the need to be a better person, to educate oneself and find happiness—it was the need to be a better son of a land, to be ready to answer not human needs in the everyday sense, but national ones in a large campaign. The rest mattered not.

It was in these days Nimrod made his first trip alone. His love of long walks, of climbing and exploring, wasn't mere curiosity as he had first thought. It was like examining a patient he'd have to cure and perhaps operate on one day, and it was living his stories, his father's stories, the Bible. The last for him wasn't Holy Scripture. It was a book he loved, and a book which was never dead, not because of the spirit of holy God hovering on the pages, but because the length and width of the country was unfolded in it, and it was a source of permanent surprise and amazement to find the places where things had happened. It was like meeting your ancestors in hidden valleys, and talking to them. So he walked.

He'd leave the village early in the mornings, leave a note saying he'd be away for a few days and walk; and he'd be David flying from Saul, and he'd be Barak preparing for war and talking to Deborah, and he'd be Solomon talking to the trees and animals.

He'd wear Arab headware, carry his shabriah and a small bag, and he'd be Joshua leading his people, and then he'd be Ivri seeing the country for the first time, and Gideon fighting, and he'd sing aloud and count the stars and he'd be Jacob. It was preparation for really being Nimrod, Nimrod the hunter, it was looking for a chance to become the additional link in the chain. And meanwhile he lived the lives and heroic stories of others. He loved his body. The hot sun helped him too, and the moon, he believed, shone on it in a special light. He grew taller and firmer, and he loved his body more than he cared for his mind or feelings. This was himself, growing, climbing, sweating. The rest was air and wind. Wind brought the rain one day, and he loved the smell of the soil after the long delayed first rain. It seemed to thank the clouds and absorb it in, and call for it and sing for it, and smell beautifully for it, and relax. The whole of creation relaxed after the rain, the farmers looked at the soil, brought back to life from heaven, and there was much work to do and no time for other things, when Lamech died.

# 9

NIMROD was working in the yard pitching hay, when
Moti, the neighbor's son, came running. "Hurry, the shoemaker is dying! They say he asked for you, quick!"

Nimrod didn't get it. "What did you say?"

"Lamech! He's dying, maybe he's dead by now!"

. . . Lamech. He is dying. Maybe he is dead by now,
Nimrod repeated. He put on a shirt, and started running.

Arriving at the cottage he saw some people around it.
He pushed them aside and went in. At first he thought the
man was dead. He was lying in the bed which was too large
for him, covered with a yellow-white sheet, eyes shut, looking pale green in the half-darkened room. The doctor was
in the room, and he indicated to Nimrod that nothing
could be done for Lamech.

Nimrod went closer to the bed, hesitating. He knew it
would happen one day, and he had thought about it, but
it was different from what he had imagined. There was a
heavy smell in the room, and no sound—the natural sounds
and noises of the village, the wind, the tractors, the human

voices, all seemed to stop, or not to be able to enter this room. And then Lamech moved. Nimrod couldn't help jumping. And then he came to the side of the bed.

"Little one," the man whispered. "Are you here?" Nimrod put his hand on Lamech's. It felt cold and hard, and he wanted to pull his own hand back so as not to touch, so as not to feel. But the old man grasped it, without strength, but with effort and will, and he was trying to talk, he thought he was talking, but no voice was heard. He couldn't open his eyes any more, and his tongue was dry and it stuck in his mouth. Finally, and almost gasping he managed to speak. "Little one," he said, "take what you want from here. It's yours when I die."

Nimrod looked at him carefully. Yet his eyes passed beyond him and rested nowhere. So that's the end, he thought, just like this. In a few minutes the hand wouldn't grasp his and the mouth would be shut like the eyes. And then there would be another tombstone on the hill, and he'd continue pitching hay. There was something heroic for him in sitting there, the boy of fourteen, tall and bright. He was the one to see Lamech die, he thought, nobody else hears what Lamech says now, and it was flattering, another secret to add to his private list. It made him feel like a man.

"Little one, are you there? Talk to me."

"Yes, Lamech. I'm here." Talk? Say what? Tell him it's all over, tell him he'll get better, say what?

"Don't mourn, Nimi, just love. You're not afraid?"

"No, Lamech. I fear nothing. Don't worry, Lamech."

"No, little one, it's not good like this. I mean . . ." And he passed away. Nimrod watched the mouth close, and then the jaw dropped, and the remaining yellow teeth showed, and the hand let go of his after a last grasp, and the doctor approached.

He pulled the sheet over the old man's face.

"You don't want to stay, Nimrod, do you? There is nothing you can do now." He did want to stay, and it wasn't out of sorrow or love for the old man who lay dead. It was merely prolonging an odd sensation, a new one, trying to drink it to the end. He knew none of his friends would have liked to stay alone with Lamech's dead body, but he knew he didn't mind. He wanted to talk to Lamech, and when the doctor left and said he'd come back in half an hour, Nimrod uncovered the upper part of the body.

Lamech had a long gown on, Nimrod saw, like an old woman's. The boy touched his hand, and then his chest and his arms. They weren't cold yet, but when he touched his own body he noticed the difference. He hesitated, he knew he shouldn't, but he touched the eyes and pulled at the lids. It was hard to do, and he stopped it. He wanted to stare at Lamech, who looked like an old roll, worn out and thrown into a corner.

"Old man, that's the end. You told me once they'd put you under a stone. This was long ago, but now they will.

"Yes, you wanted me to love and dance and sing, but Ivri says these things will not save the country. And neither will praying. Yes, Ivri is right. He said you were jealous of him. And now you're dead, and what is left? This body left to the worms. This little cottage. I might visit from time to time, a new shoemaker will come to make sandals and boots, and yours will be thrown out after a time. What? I shouldn't talk like this? What shall I tell you, Lamech? You asked me to talk, and so I talk. Soon the doctor will come and they'll wash you. Did you ever wash? All your body? They'll make you clean, and I'll go to cemetery hill. You won't tell me stories any more. But I don't want to listen to stories any more. You say I pretend? I do? Hell, that's the way I feel, old man.

"We're going to have a war soon. You can't tell any stories about the war, you're too good for that. You're too good for us all. I know you're better than Gideon and Ivri and myself. I could never dance alone on the hill, and I know you never lied and you loved us all.

"Ivri said I should have no friends, so I kept away from you too. Yes, true Lamech, you are a friend . . ."

"Who on earth are you talking to, boy?"

It was the doctor coming back. "Oh, to Lamech," he said and quickly recovered the corpse.

"Does he answer, the old man?"

"Sure he does. What are you going to do with him?"

"Nothing for little children to watch. He's going to be washed and cleaned and prepared and we'll bury him tomorrow morning."

We'll bury him tomorrow morning.

Bury him.

We'll bury Lamech—tomorrow morning. He could sing it.

He could take what he wanted from the cottage. Did he want anything? There were tools useless to him. He picked them up one after the other and then put them back. Useless. Maybe the new shoemaker could use them.

He looked at the clock, the few clothes, the shirts, an overcoat. Useless. His mother would say they were dirty and throw them out. He took the watch. It was hung on a silver chain, and had stopped ticking long ago. "What's the time? What difference does it make?" Lamech had said a long time ago. And still he carried the watch in his trouser pocket. Nimrod took it. Lamech was right about time, he thought. It's time to eat, or sleep, or do something or stop doing something. But it isn't the watch that points it out, it's one's body.

It was then that he really realized that Lamech was dead. Almost without knowing what he was doing he sat on the wooden floor and started playing with the scraps of leather, collecting them and talking aloud, not noticing that it was growing darker. This one looks like a tree, and these are rocks, and that's the head of a bull, and this is—just the tail of a cat. And the square one—well, it's like a yellow stone in the cemetery. Yellow stones, yellow teeth, almost yellow hair. He thought it would be right to put a square of leather on Lamech's tomb instead of a stone one.

He collected the scraps into one paper bag, and into another one, and, leaving the door open, he went home.

"You were crying!" Miriam said.

"Oh no. Lamech died."

"I know. I'm sorry. The old man liked you. But you were crying."

"Maybe. I didn't notice. Where can I put my leather?"

"Your what?"

"Just a souvenir from Lamech. Can I put it in the upper shelf on the cupboard?"

"Do you want to keep these little scraps? You needn't. The man is dead. You can keep one or two, but— All right, boy! You're your own master. Put them wherever you want to."

"Did you know Lamech before he came here?"

"No. They said he was a rabbi, and he decided to live close to the soil and left everything behind. They also said he was once very rich and left his home when young to come here, but nobody really knows."

"Who will take the cottage now?"

"I don't know. We'll find a new shoemaker soon. Maybe he'll be nice, Nimrod, and you'll like him, and you'll be able to go over and talk with him."

"Maybe."

That evening, late, Nimrod went to Gideon's house. Somehow Lamech's death reminded him of Gideon, shapeless and tied to his bed like Lamech in his last moments. Gideon used to be the opposite of everything Lamech represented and was, and now, with one dead, and the other very ill and wounded, they were so alike, so close, belonging to each other.

"Are you asleep?" Nimrod inquired from the corridor.

"Nimi! Come, please, you're a blessing. Here, come near, you can sit on the bed. You were crying?" Gideon's head was still bandaged but he could see, and his strong brown eyes were the only feature that hadn't changed.

"Yes, Gideon. Lamech is dead."

It was the wrong thing to say.

Gideon pulled the blanket over him though it was hot, and sank into silence.

Nimrod waited a few moments.

"Gideon?"

He came closer. "Gideon?" The man was weeping. He had never seen Gideon crying like this, sobbing, almost shaking.

"What is it?" He never even suspected Gideon could cry like this, and he knew he didn't care much for Lamech. Nimrod was crying too.

"He was better than us, Nimi. He had a God. What do I have? No hands, no legs, no head, not the slightest will to go on living except for living death.

"He died with a smile, I'm sure. I can see him now. I'll

die struggling and go nowhere, because I don't believe there is anywhere to go to." He was still sobbing and he held Nimrod's hand. Odd, the boy thought, how the hand feels like Lamech's before his death, a needing hand, helpless and desperate.

"He had a God, and all I have is pity. Even you, you loved Lamech more than you care for me. It's true, isn't it?"

"Yes, Gideon. He was different, strange."

"You remember when he took you to the pink house and I was angry? I was jealous. I've never been there, and I was curious and wanted to go. I wanted to pray at times, and I never would because it wasn't suitable for the Rock to go to the pink house, or pray or believe in God. The Rock had to be the example, the new type, the strong and fearless, and he wasn't to fear God.

"And now I can't walk all the way to the pink house, and God won't come to me. God went to Lamech's cottage when he died, I know it."

"Relax, Gideon. You'll be exhausted, don't let it upset you. The old man is dead and we go on living, and you'll be all right. I'll show you my leather scraps one day. They make funny shapes."

"Promise you will?"

"I do. I swear."

"When will they bury him?"

"They'll bury Lamech in the morning."

Bury Lamech. Bury Lamech in the morning, near the secret meeting place, and they'll put a yellow stone above him so he'll never be able to get out.

Bury Lamech in the morning.

# 10

THEY buried Lamech.

The war started and Nimrod was only fourteen. He knew the war would start, and the series of incidents in 1947 brought an end to the tension and a beginning to a total war.

The night the state was declared and established was an odd one.

They were sitting, like other thousands, near the wireless sets, and they heard the news, and it swept over them all.

Beit-On woke up, and women in gowns, and men and children, all ran to the village theater. A couple of harmonicas, an accordion, and dancing—dozens of legs dancing the hora. And singing. No words. Just songs. They knew that the next day they'd go to win, they knew it was a start and not an end, and their legs swept the wooden floor, their faces lit with expressions which included pride and joy and hope and deep knowledge of what was going to be. They danced, and it was sacred. Ivri took Miriam and danced, and he was crying. He, Motl, the son of Rabbi

Pimchas, in Beit-On, the valley above the lake, he had a state, so it wasn't in vain, nothing was in vain. They were all lifted as if by magic, the floor and the building, the whole village seemed to be somewhere high up, as high as the highest tree, and they had an expression as if they were lifted and would never be dropped, would win, and would never lose, somewhere high up.

Nimrod went out. He was high up too, but too busy with himself to get involved in the general gaiety. So he walked to see places.

He passed near the pink house. Not that he went in there, for after Lamech took him he never went there. But he passed by, and there was light.

There never was light in the pink house at night, and he was curious and opened the door. He had no cap on, and wouldn't go in, but there were people there. The old people of Beit-On, they didn't dance, neither did they sleep. They were praying. Nimrod listened—the song overpowered the prayer—he could hear

> "We came to the country
> to build it, and be built in it"

from the theater, and the low murmur of voices of the elders in the pink house—"God have mercy on us. God, and We"—and the sky was moonless and wouldn't answer or choose, and the lake, a dark pool below, so dark in color, was almost frightening, and for a minute, when the song stopped there was WE. Nimrod closed the door. They didn't notice him, and he went on. He was slightly annoyed with himself, or rather with his age. He was so young. He could shoot, but he wondered whether they'd let him take part. And if they didn't? What would he do, he, the Rock, stay home with the women and kids, with the old ones and invalids? Invalids? He thought of Gideon, and changed his direction. He'd go to Gideon. Where would he be? He couldn't walk away, and maybe he was asleep, and maybe he was listening to the songs. Gideon would talk to him and understand.

He found him outside, on the pavement opposite his path. He was crying like a baby, but this happened to him often. Gideon had heard the news, and seen the village gathering, and he got up, and with all the strength left in his amputated paralyzed body he started to join the others, and he got this far. He was lying on the soil, playing with its grains with his healthy hand, and his tears mixed with the earth, and he listened.

He thought, I have no right to live like this, to be a burden and of no use, and now there would be a battle, a long and bloody battle, and where would the Rock be? Here on the ground. Not to get up, and not to be able to walk, and it's painful even to be like this on and on. So, where to? It isn't life, neither is it quitting, and if I hear the noise of planes and tanks and am stuck in this cottage. . . . He hated his cottage, and the lawn, and the white color of the houses and his bandages. He listened to the boys and wanted to shout—Sing, you fools, tomorrow you might be killed or what's worse, tomorrow you might be lying in the dust like me. He pulled himself and managed to get up. He wasn't unhappy. His real tears were those of joy and pride, only there was a difference between the knowledge that he'd done his part, and contributed his share and the emotional recognition of a coming war during which he'd have to lie down, he, Gideon, "fighter" as they called him in his unit, he, the Rock. It was bitterness, jealousy; he was like a woman discovering she had flirted with the wrong person, and was too tired when her real lover came, and here came the demand of Gideon's love and he was impotent. He felt bitter, and then self-piteous and exhausted when Nimrod came.

The boy didn't speak. He joined Gideon on the pavement and let him take his hand.

"Happy, Nimi?"

"Yes. I think so. It's confusing to get something you've wanted all the time, and yet to have to stand almost aside when fighting for it."

"What should I say then?"

"You did your share. They won't tell me I'm too young, will they?"

"But you are. There is much to do besides fighting. It is as important to keep the village going as to fight a battle. Many of the men will be away, and you kids will have to carry on with the farms, take care of the young children. Oh, there will be much to do."

Nimrod felt it wasn't a compensation. It was like blowing up a balloon and then not letting it fly, and the same people who blew it wouldn't let it free.

"Help me in, boy." Nimrod let Gideon lean on him and they went inside. "Close the door. The windows too! I can't stand the singing! Why aren't you there anyway?"

"I was. I just went out to get some air. Everybody is there. Do you mind if I stay?"

"Yes!" Gideon almost shouted. It was sudden jealousy. He knew Nimrod could give his share. He knew he now deserved the name "Rock" instead of himself, and one day he'd be "Fighter." The boy was healthy, and intelligent, he'd never make his own mistake, never be hurt stupidly—

—or maybe yes.

"Hey, Nimi. Just a moment. Say. You're not afraid of things, are you?"

"No!" Nimrod knew now. He wasn't. He felt strange about it as he didn't think he liked being this way. He knew some of his friends were like this, not brave, but lacking feeling. Places, situations where he knew he should have been afraid, he just didn't feel anything, no reaction, no sensation, not any more the feeling in his stomach and his feet, not a shiver. He couldn't explain it, because it hadn't always been like this, and he couldn't reason it either. Was it due to Ivri's treatment? Or Lamech's, or a reaction to Lamech? The children around? The pulse of the country? It grew with his body, with his love of the country, with his impudence—and the fears disappeared with the disappearance of the rabbit from his shelf—with its being tucked away somewhere, with Lamech taken from his life. Was it the work he was doing, his frequent walks, and his being alone which gave him self-assurance and self-knowledge? He couldn't tell. He had no sense of humor, and there was no self-criticism. He understood whatever he did well, and had an overdeveloped sense of pride. But the wrong things, they were pushed away or covered with excuses like—it was necessary, or—it's a result of being strong, or—it's needed for the good of this course or another; losing self-criticism meant losing sensitivity and things wore the uniform of black and white only.

Life was physical for Nimrod, his joys were physical, and his demands the same. His purpose was a permanent proof of physical potency, ability, maturity. His lack of humor made it complex as he wouldn't take things easy and would refuse to admit or recognize failure.

The other Nimrod, who wasn't so much—the new type, slowly took refuge and hid. He appeared in dreams sometimes, in lonely trips when he could afford loving the scenery and allowing himself the emotional luxury of picking flowers and forgetting his body. But it never went as far as to fear something, this was pushed under the weight of the rest, neglected, forbidden, and left to rust and change color. Even his previous fear of being afraid disappeared and became a subconscious thing, and he was slowly turning into a man, taking Gideon's place, and while Gideon the Rock slowly turned into a little Rock, and then into a potential Lamech, Nimrod was now the Rock.

Only he hadn't had a chance to prove it, and the war refused to give him one. He was too young, and he did remain in the village, and when the war was over, and the state well established he was a leader without an army, a balloon which hadn't flown, an unfulfilled woman.

Gideon became smaller, shrinking with years and medicines, and his color changed. He never left the house and friends seldom went to see him. He started writing poetry, not good poetry, but sad, full of self-pity and admiration— to an unknown God. He wrote about weeds forming a crown to his heart, about his mother's milk being sour and his father's whip being too short and made of cotton wool. He wrote about sunsets and flowers and his talk was like this.

"You've changed, Gideon. I find I have nothing in common with you," said Nimrod, who still used to visit him on occasions.

"Oh no. I've always been like this. You are changing, Nimi. Maybe you can't help it."

"I like it," boasted Nimrod. "I'm not Nimi any more, and I like it."

"You do. You like yourself. I used to, it was my body I liked, apparently, as when it was gone, I didn't like myself as much. As a matter of fact, I detested myself."

"Have you written anything new—"

"Shall I read you something?"

Nimrod didn't mind Gideon's poetry. There was something sad in it, and moving, even when he didn't understand or agree, and he knew Gideon wanted to read it. So he listened.

"My soul left my body
and looked back in hatred.
It flew away
to pick snow from the Chermon,
to pick red flowers from the hill
and a piece of sky
and lay them down on my body's grave.
My soul wept and mocked it,
and wished never to return,
and my God pushed it back
and made it stay, and be buried,
with the snow and flowers and sky."

It went on like this. There were pages and pages of it, and Nimrod thought of other things when he listened or pretended to. And then he would thank Gideon and walk away. If he had ever liked Gideon's company, now he felt only pity, sorrow, and a sense of waste. It was a waste of time, waste of attention, waste of days and hours of life for Gideon to go on living. Yet, he did, and clutched to life and to his God of snow and flowers and sky. And Nimrod's was iron and stone, but he knew that somewhere he shared a God with Gideon.

# 11

THE tall man put on his trousers and white shirt; he
didn't tuck his shirt inside the trousers because he thought
it looked better this way. He poured some water on his hair
and combed it. But when he looked at the mirror he
thought it was too orderly, and he moved his fingers
through it to give it a more natural look. Once again he
stroked his cheek to make sure that he didn't need a shave.
He seldom needed a shave, because hardly any hair grew
on his face. A once-a-week treatment was all he needed.
Yet, every morning he asked himself—"Do I need a shave?"

Now where were his sandals? "Miriam," he called. "Did
you see my sandals?" He preferred to call his mother by
her name—it made him feel older. Miriam entered the
room and stood next to Nimrod. He was only seventeen
and yet he was much taller than she was. She was proud
of him. In a short while he'd be a soldier, and yet she still
thought of him as Nimi, although Ivri and the boy
wouldn't let her call him that. Nimrod scared her. It was
not what he did. It was his reactions. Sometimes she'd

think, "It can't be true, it's inhuman and impossible." He didn't care deeply about anything these last few years since the war. She knew he felt frustrated because he hadn't taken part in the war. But he was only a boy then, and yet he would push her away whenever she tried to hug and kiss him. Now he had a new kind of smile, a smile of mockery and sadness and odd superiority which he smeared on his face and which never indicated what was happening underneath.

He had no friends and he worked hard. He was sociable, he went to meetings and was liked, but he had no friends. What frightened her was that he didn't seem to need people.

He had a great love for the country. He frequently took long trips and walks, and she knew he would do anything for it. Only it had become an urgency for him to do something, and if there wasn't anything feasible to do he'd invent something.

Ivri, on the other hand, watched all this with growing pride and pleasure. Nimrod was taller and stronger than he, and he knew what was demanded of him. After so many years it was good to be able to depend on somebody else, to transfer responsibility to someone so capable and reliable. The boy didn't need guidance any more. He was independent and self-sufficient, and so they were to let him alone, never interfering, never demanding or even asking, and each of them living in his own circle of hard work, hard living, and worries.

Miriam didn't ask him where he was going. She never did. She smiled at the way he had dressed up and brushed his hair. She found his sandals for him. He said shalom and left. It was late in the evening.

They were to meet the girls that night. A group of recently arrived immigrants from Hungary who were staying in the village to learn the language and get some training wanted to meet the boys of Beit-On. The girls were a year or so older than Nimrod's group, but they all met that evening in the youth cottage and sat together on the grass outside.

When there are no words, there are songs. So the boys started singing. The girls, still frightened and shy, all seemed to look the same to Nimrod—blond, fair-skinned, their hair combed back—and he kept staring at them, as did the other boys.

The girl whom he liked most was sitting opposite him. She was very small, and she looked about fourteen. She had long hair, the color of wheat, tied tightly back, and he couldn't decide what the color of her eyes was. Nimrod didn't care much for girls, mainly because there weren't many in the village. But he thought he knew how to deal with them, having watched Ivri and Miriam. And having a girl friend and marrying eventually were all more or less natural expected things, leading to the having of a son or sons. He never thought of girls as women, or as creatures that differed very much from him. They were companions, but slightly weaker and in need of defense. If they were clever you could talk to them, but this seldom happened.

Perhaps Nimrod was atracted to the girl because she paid no attention to him. And when she did he felt put on the defensive.

"You looked at me," she said. "What's your name?"

"Nimrod."

"I like your hair," she said. Nobody ever said things like that to him, and she had no right to either. He wanted to say something to her to make her feel small, but he didn't.

"It used to be curly once."

"A pity. I like curly hair. It's usually softer, but I like yours too."

She and Miriam. Females both. They liked curly hair. He regretted that his hair wasn't curly any more and he hated himself for regretting.

She was leading the conversation; he followed. Her Hebrew wasn't good but she tried very hard, and he found her mistakes charming.

"You can teach me Hebrew," she said.

He didn't want to teach anybody, but he said, "Yes, I will. What's your name?"

"Elli."

"How old are you?"

"Twenty."

So she was older than he. She looked so young. She was small, and yet she was much older, and he knew she had gone through so much more than he had.

He asked her if he could see her home. He didn't really want to, he thought, but she was small and helpless, and he might as well.

They left the others and walked toward the girls' cottage. She put her hand on his arm, leaned on it. He froze for a second. What did she want of him? Why would she put her hand on his? What was he to do? She talked, about her home and childhood and how happy she was to come here.

"I like the people, and I love the country here, and it's all so different and new."

She talked like Ivri, he thought, she talked about the new youth in the new country.

"Were you in the war?" she asked.

He didn't like that question. He had to tell her he was young, or else he had to lie. He couldn't lie. He never did these days, or needed to.

"No, Elli. I wasn't. They wouldn't let me. I'm very young, you see, and I was a young boy during the war. But it's not over. I'm joining the army soon." He found himself talking. And somehow he started talking about Gideon.

"Will you take me to see him?"

"Why do you want to?"

"He is your friend. And besides I think I will like him."

She thinks she'll like Gideon. How does she know, and why does she smile all the time, but not with her eyes? Her eyes roved over objects, resting nowhere, and finally staring into the distance. He didn't like it. When he looked at something he nailed objects to a spot, pierced them through and was definite and precise. She was vague and mysterious. She had no right to be like that.

She was still holding his arm. Once, when she stumbled she grasped it, and his muscle hardened. She felt it.

"You are strong. Your arm is very strong. I like it."

Now he was proud. She had noticed.

"I could lift you high up, like a child or a feather."

"No, you couldn't. I'm heavier than you think."

He lifted her, his hands holding her by the waist, and he could feel her body, smooth and bony. She gasped when he lifted her, and smiled. He held her up. Never had he been that close to a girl, and now there she was, her hair like a crown, and her skirt against his white shirt. And she felt so light that he knew he could walk on and on with her forever like this.

"No, let me down, Nimrod," she said. "I'm heavy."

He did, slowly, pausing when her face was opposite his and looking her straight in the eye. And he put her down carefully, as if she were made of delicate glass.

It was like a new toy, but the reaction of his body was strange and new and exciting. He shivered, and he felt a strong desire to hold her tight, and, embarrassed by the idea, an urge to run away. And now she was crying. All of a sudden, just before they reached the cottage, Elli was weeping and Nimrod knew what to do. He was the strong and confident one.

He stroked her hair and asked her why she cried. He knew that was the right thing to do. He held her face in his hands and asked her why, and asked if he could do anything for her. He had never seen a girl crying, had never seen Miriam cry. She was like a small baby and he liked it, puzzling as it was.

"Elli, do you want anything?"

"The moon," she said. "Only the moon," and laughed, and he noticed in the dark that when she cried the smile was still there and she didn't talk.

"I'll get you the moon. That's easy. We'll go to the lake one night and you'll see it in the water and I'll dive in and fish it out for you. Would you like me to do that?"

"Yes, Nimrod. I'm sorry. I'm happy."

"So why do you cry?" He wanted to say nice things to her, for he didn't understand her and it was all beautiful. But he didn't know any nice things to say, so he lifted her up again, high up, and held her close, and then let her down.

"You see how light you are! You should eat and eat and eat until I can't lift you any more."

She wasn't crying now. She was laughing and her laughter was sweet in the dark, and she was holding his hand.

"See how big your hand is! Twice the size of mine. That's why I cried."

"I don't understand, Elli."

"I can't explain in Hebrew. It's the first time I am not afraid, and feel protected, and the first time I cry, not because of something terrible or cruel or sad, but because I want to make the moment last. You are so clean and straight. I never met people like you before."

"You like me?" He thought he wasn't being himself that night. What business did he have to stand like this with a girl he didn't know and older than himself, and ask her questions, and make her cry, and lift her like this?

"Yes, Nimrod, I like you. Do you want to kiss me?"

Did he want to kiss her? He looked at her lips. They were parted and pink and rather thin, and he felt his own lips with his tongue but couldn't remember what they looked like. He wasn't sure how he should kiss her or why, so he nodded and waited.

She stood up on her toes and held his face and put her lips on his, and he held her in his arms. She was still shivering—or was it he? And he kissed her the way he used to kiss his mother when he was a boy, but she still held him and he did it again, and then she was pushing her tongue between his lips and drinking him in.

He did the same. He was scared he might hurt her, and he tried to be tender and delicate, but he felt her body next to his, very near, and in kissing her breathed it all in. He was afraid to move his hands or his head, and only his lips moved, and his tongue, and he stopped thinking and let his body relax, and it was like a stream going through it, vigorous and rolling and demanding, and he felt stiff and funny, almost embarrassed, and he separated himself from her.

"Have you kissed a woman before?" she asked. A woman, she said. Nobody used this word in the village. Even Miriam was called a girl, and she said a woman. She was a woman. He was a man.

"No, you are the first one, Elli. And I liked it."

They parted.

She had said he could protect her, and he wanted to, and she had cried because she was happy, and maybe he made her happy.

She had felt his muscles and his strength, and he knew he was strong.

He imagined himself coming back from a war, and there would be Elli to receive him and admire him. She was a woman, she said so herself, and he had kissed her mouth and held her body close. The body of a woman, and his body felt it. He was glad she had gone away and left him with the memory and sensation and hope, and he strolled along whistling and feeling as light as Elli was. He still couldn't remember the color of her eyes. Next time he'd look carefully.

# 12

NIMROD avoided Elli for the next few days but it was only because he was confused. He dreamed about her body night after night, and ate her with his bread, drank her with his water. He wanted to tell the whole world about Elli. He wanted to yell her name from the roofs and call her from the top of the Chermon. Yet whenever he saw her near the girls' cottage he was overcome by shyness and passed by, pretending he didn't see her.

And then one night she came over.

They were all sitting on the terrace, and not a word was being spoken. It was one of those green-blue evenings when you just listen to the sounds of nature and your body seems to be nailed to the chair, your hands heavy and your tongue bound, and all you want to do is sit forever and try to distinguish the sound of the grasshoppers from that of the frogs. Listen—a dog barking far away, a car on the main road, the radio next door. Listen more carefully—no, no wind tonight. A mosquito somewhere in the air, your own pulse beating, counting the seconds toward the unknown

future—yet scorning it. Three people together yet separated, each wrapped in himself, beyond thinking, beyond
thought. Even the wind seemed to die away at moments
like this.

And then Elli appeared.

There was something dreadfully different about her.
She came as if from another world, and the three people
noticed it. The terrace came to life. Nimrod introduced
her, watching his mother's surprise and his father's curiosity. There was something clean about Elli. She was smiling,
but they weren't. She was smiling the way they thought
one shouldn't, a meaningless smile, a smile without reason.
She smiled because she was happy and loving and rather
tired, and she took a chair and relaxed, still clean and smiling and remote.

She was wearing a white dress and sandals, and her hair
was tied back as before, and now Nimrod could see the
color of her eyes. They were green, or hazel, or a mixture
of both, but there was green in them, and her skin was fair,
almost untouched by the sun, and so were her long fingers
and legs.

They started talking. Fast, suddenly, to drown the sounds
of nature, to drown the silence and the embarrassment.

"I was passing by and I wanted to say hello. I wondered
if you'd join me for a walk," said Elli to Nimrod.

"How nice of you," said Miriam. "But please have something to eat before you go. I'll fix something!"

It was Miriam's wonderful escape—the kitchen, the
cup of tea, where she could stand and watch the water
boiling, listen to the movement in the kettle, watch the
steam gathering on the low ceiling, and let her unhurried
thoughts flow with the steam and hover above the stove.

"Nice girl," she thought, "but strange. A pretty girl, one of the Hungarian group. . . . Would Nimrod marry a new immigrant? Such a gap in habits, concepts, manners, and ideas. But why not if it'll make him happy." She cut some bread, and set a pitcher of fresh cream and olives and boiled eggs on a tray. The tea was ready now and she had to go back to the terrace.

Miriam always felt sorry when she left the kitchen, when she had to go out and talk and listen. And this was Ivri's fault. He had placed her there, with love and affection, placed her near the boiling water and the white sink turned yellow with the years.

Elli was telling about her farming experiences. She spoke with humor, lightly, laughing at her own mistakes, talking fluently, pausing from time to time on a serious note or in search of a word.

Ivri was listening, not to Nimrod's friend, but to the new immigrant in her, and Nimrod was just watching her. He couldn't get used to her mere presence, there, on the terrace, white and smiling. He couldn't talk or answer. This was Elli, in his house. He wanted to say things to her, he wanted to own her. He felt he shouldn't share her with his parents like this. When she had had her tea he stood up.

"Our walk, Elli. It's getting late."

She thanked Miriam, shook hands with Ivri, and got up.

"Come again," Miriam said.

"Good luck!" Ivri added, seriously, and they left.

"I had to see you," Elli apologized when they were alone. "I thought you were cross with me, or that I had done something wrong."

"No, Elli. I was busy," he lied. "I'll have more time this week. Come along whenever you want to."

"Show me your village, master! Show me the places you like, the corners you wove dreams in, the rock upon which you sat and planned your life. I'm yours!"

She was strangely gay. Nimrod was more and more confused. She spoke the way Gideon wrote. He too used to think in these terms, but no more.

"This is the armory," he said. "Now it's legal and operating openly. When I was very young it was a secret, disguised as a workshop and it had a cellar where the arms were kept."

"Let's get away from the square. These things were said to us on our first day. The 'get acquainted' tour, you know."

Again she held his arm and the same shiver went through him. They took the path leading to the hill and King's Forest.

"Now I want a flower!"

"Yes!" He was happy to do something for her. He picked a flower and handed it to her as if it were made of delicate glass.

"Lift me again, Nimrod!"

"Not now. When we reach the top of the hill!"

It was a bright night and they could see the hills clearly, the trees like swords thrust into the sky and the lake like frozen ice with a crown of lights from the settlements around it.

When they reached the forest Elli was tired. Her eyes were shining and her hands were wet.

He chose a rock, and they relaxed against it. He untied the ribbon and let her hair fall on her shoulders, yellow against the white dress, and he stroked it lightly. Only then did he feel how rough his hands were. Her hair tickled him.

He pushed her down on the grass.

"Please," she said, "don't hurt me." And then she said something in Hungarian.

He didn't listen. It was all sudden and bursting. He had felt weak and gentle and childish sitting and stroking her hair, and then his body screamed yes, and his body was his master. He forgot the forest and the lake and the village below. She had said before she was a woman, not a girl. And here he was, a man, the Rock.

He kissed her on her lips and on her neck, and his hands held her lightly and moved along her body. He forgot her name and her color and her looks, and he didn't want to remember. His hands were moving there, along the curves of her body, and he opened the buttons and searched, discovering, creating, being the first man with the first woman. He was heavy on her, he knew. He didn't mind. He'd be heavy on her and she'd be his. She'd stop smiling and being poetic. She'd just be his. He wanted to hurt her. He touched her leg, and the grass under it, and he moved his hands up to touch her warm stomach and found her breast. He could tear and destroy. He thought she was talking to him but he didn't answer. Her hands touched his body, he thought, but it was him, his body, his legs, his organs and breath and lips and arms. He opened his shirt and helped her out of her frock. Her skin shone like ivory and she was cold. He wouldn't stop, because if he stopped he'd run far away, and he could almost hear the old echo—show us you're strong, strong, strong.

His hands dug hard into her hair. But when his lips touched her breast he was a baby again and his muscles relaxed. And so he moved, being both a baby and an animal, going to pieces for a moment, being a mountain and a rock again, and then a child in the cradle. But it was only he. She wasn't there.

Until his hand touched her wetness. And then he shuddered and went into her. She cried. The minute he touched her he felt his body being thrown out of his skin and scattered in the air. And then he came out and rolled on his back, and let his hands fall to the sides of his body. And he was a child again.

Now he wanted to disappear, to shrink to the size of an egg and be washed and put in a small box.

Elli was lying, her eyes open, staring vaguely into nothing, and she was weeping, slowly. She knew he didn't notice that she was there. She knew it wasn't she, Elli. It was a woman, any woman, and he just wanted to be a man. She felt that if she'd get up and go, he wouldn't notice. But she liked it.

It was the first time she had given herself completely, the first time she was physical only and nothing else, the first time words didn't matter and poetic images didn't exist. The animal in her was there. She liked being hurt, and he had hurt her. She feared him, and feared his violence, but it was an unknown part, belonging there, and she felt the soil under her and the grass, and she was cold and wet and it was good.

"Talk to me," she implored.

He did not. He was hardly there.

"Please, Nimrod, talk to me. Say something, anything." She kissed him and touched his hair, and he did not move.

He opened his eyes, stared at her, and shut his eyes.

"I hurt you," he said at last.

She smiled. "No, that's you. You didn't mean to. I know you can be gentle and tender. It just happened this way. I feel fine."

"I hurt you. I am too strong for you."

"I love your strength. I really feel fine. I'm cold."

He didn't listen. She said she loved his strength. He touched his own body, and felt guilty for a second when his hand got wet, felt like a baby again. She said he could be gentle and tender. He didn't care to be. He wanted to be a storm, not a breeze, and he opened his eyes again.

"Were you afraid?" he asked her.

"Yes. But only for a moment. Now I am cold."

He stood up, walked a few steps, and leaned against a tree. She tied her hair. Her white dress was wrinkled and didn't look as clean as before.

He became joyous.

"Come! I'll show you my village, little Elli. I'll show you my corners and rocks and secret places. Here! You're standing on one. Here I first loved a woman!"

"Don't use this word 'love,' please," she begged.

He went on. "Here I first loved a woman, a journey into manhood, short and intensive, and from now on this is your secret corner too, your first one in Beit-On. Now," he said, and there was cruelty in his voice, "I'll take you to my two friends. One probably never had a woman, and there is a stone weighing on his dead body, and the second will never have a woman again because he has no body. We're going!"

She wasn't quite sure what she felt. There was something superior about Nimrod, but she didn't know how positive this superiority was. For a moment he was God, a God of nature and health, and a second after he was a helpless babe, a little monster, a poet and then again he was the Lord. The notes of cruelty in his voice hurt her. He was humorous, but only concerning others, and she felt he couldn't sense things and their extreme delicacy.

He was walking in front of her, silent, relaxed, leading

the way to the cemetery. They were going to visit Lamech, he said, to say good night, a permanent good night, never good morning any more.

And Elli followed. For Nimrod death was an emphasis on life. For her—a loss, and another one, and then another one, and as their concepts were so far apart she couldn't even be angry or upset. She believed the child in Nimrod felt otherwise, and maybe sensed the loss. Elli thought graveyards should be dug in the desert or in the rocks, without plants and flowers around. She thought people should sense death, and let it infiltrate and invade them when they were near graves, and indicate where they stood and what life was worth. Instead, she thought, moving now among the graves following Nimrod, you see the plants, the green overcoming the yellow, and you see the trees, ancient and rooted and healthy, and you are given false hopes and are filled with life.

Nimrod was filled with himself, a sense of achievement which always drove him into a satanic mood.

"A flower for my queen!" he said, "raised and grown on human flesh, like ours. The flesh died, gave life to the soil, gave birth to the flower, which is given to you—to perish and die again!"

He lifted her again, and kissed her.

"Here! The old man, my second father, the maker of shoes, sandals, boots, fairy tales, toy rabbits, and dreams. If the place was lit you could read on the stone—'Rabbi Lamech from Kiev, born date unknown, died 1950, May his soul rest in peace.'"

And then something happened to Nimrod. He lost his silly smile and tone of mockery, and held his head in his hands, bending over for a moment as if he would faint, and Elli had to let him lean against her.

"What is it, dear?" she asked softly. "Come, let's move on and sit for a moment."

"I don't know. My head. I am too much for myself at times. I'm sorry. I'll be fine in a few seconds."

"Talk to me, Nimrod."

"I'd like to. I can't. I don't mean to mock old Lamech. He meant so much to me, only I can't forgive myself for my behavior the last few years of his life. There was so much sadness when he looked at me, not believing in me any more, and the sadder he grew the happier I became, more teasing, cynical, proving. I can't talk about it. It's the same with you, you see. You're better than me, as Lamech was."

"You look so scared, Nimrod. Please talk more."

"No, Elli, I'm not. I'm just disgusted and appalled with myself, but this will pass too."

"I can't imagine you really scared. You're so strong. We all have moments of weakness and wrongs, but I like you enough to go through them with you. You're a new and strange type for me. I'll get used to you."

"It's getting very late. We can pass by and see if there is a light at Gideon's and say good night to him and go home. Here. Your hand!"

Gideon's cottage was dark, and in the shadows of the trees look darker than the other houses. They decided to walk around it and see if there was a light in the back, and while doing so they heard a voice.

"Over here, kids. The object you're looking for"—Elli frowned—"is laid on the lawn to enjoy the fresh air and the company of insects. Good evening."

Gideon's body was stretched out on a blanket, leaning on a pillow at the edge of the lawn at the back of the white house—all houses in Beit-On were whitewashed.

"This is Elli, Gideon; Elli wanted to meet you."

"I am not my best little self tonight," Gideon said. "I'm wearing the costume. It's a game we play—the plaster and bandages and all. Tomorrow morning I'll be out of it."

Nimrod cut in. "Stop it, you fool. She knows better. She wanted to hear poems. Stop making fun of yourself and playing games."

"So, she wants to hear poems. Another heart full of pity and understanding. It lasts one meeting, another one is a result of guilt, and a third to explain how busy one is these days, and then eternity."

"My Hebrew is very bad," said Elli softly, "so I can't answer you fast. My father was an invalid the last few years of his life, and I couldn't understand you better. I know how killing pity is, and I feel none for you, no more than I pity myself or anybody."

Gideon took it in, said nothing, but relaxed for a moment.

"She is pretty, Nimrod," he observed. "Are you two in love? Well, I shouldn't ask," he noticed that they blushed, "but that's what Nimrod needs, to love. Nimi! Would you go in and bring the beer out. I do feel like a cold drink."

"You call him Nimi?"

"Yes. Silly, too. Never did before I was wounded. If you have time one day do come over. I'll tell you about your man as a child. This was before he became the Rock, when his hair was curly and he was small and weak; he wouldn't want to remember it now. One day it'll be the only thing he'll have to cling to, but if you care to listen come any time. I'm always at home."

"I'd love to. I like him as he is now. I wouldn't want him to be different—but I'd love to listen."

Nimrod returned with the bottles.

# 13

NIMROD called it being in love, and as definitions have no value unless we feel them deeply—it was love.

He knew very little about Elli, which didn't matter much as it was he who was in love, and the feeling, the experience, and the novelty of it filled him. He loved to love the way he did, and the object of his love happened to be Elli.

She saw in him what he saw in himself. She was strange and new and this added to his feeling that he was doing something good by loving her. And as days passed and the farm demanded much work, and there were several border clashes and many other things to think about, his emotions were simplified. There was Elli, and there was he, and he loved her because he kissed her, and walked with her, and made love to her, and shared small unimportant things with her, and she returned his feeling.

Nimrod was receiving it all, and taking it for granted. It never occurred to him it might be changed or altered. If she was sad or disappointed at times, this was her problem. He was not sensitive or too delicate about matters of the heart, and enjoyed being a clean dish into which love and attentions were poured, ever to be consumed and ready to be refilled.

One day Elli went to visit Gideon alone. She had meant to go for a long time and yet she was somehow frightened. She put up with the limited communication she achieved with Nimrod, and didn't want to disturb it.

So maybe it was the late spring clouds, or the fact that she had a free day, or a small quarrel with Nimrod the night before. Anyhow she went to see Gideon.

He was in one of his difficult days. Sulky, closed into himself, sunk into indifference, not willing to breathe the fresh air of the alive world. And Elli was a representative of this alive world, and he wouldn't let her in.

She knocked politely on the door.

"Not now. Who is it anyway?"

"Me, Elli, Nimi's friend. I want to talk to you."

"No! You should go away. You pity me again. I'm busy now."

She hesitated, put her palm on the knob, and didn't move it.

"Please, let me talk to you. Don't act with me."

"Go away. If you want to hear about Nimrod, go to the spring. That's the meeting place of the kids. You'll see your man's childhood, and your son's future. I'm busy. Go now."

The spring? The kids? She would do that. She let go of the knob and turned away.

Gideon moved inside the house, holding to the wall, the chairs, the small ladder, the door. This path he knew and detested—depending on it as he did. He opened the door a crack, and peeped out. He could see Elli's yellow hair and her blue shirt and shorts, and the legs of a very young girl wearing sandals. He slammed the door hard. The movement tired him. He wanted to be dead tired, to cease to feel, to just let it ache real bad and drown himself in the pain and forget the rest of it.

Now back to the armchair—the door—the small ladder —the chairs. So first back to the small ladder, and with his one hand he pushed it hard. It fell on the floor and lay leaning against the door like a fallen barricade. The noise was less than he had expected but somehow it soothed him. He liked breaking or pushing things. The sound would invade his veins with the pain, and he'd feel his mind disintegrating, and the whole of his entity would be a million cells each filled with sound and pain.

He knew he'd have to beg someone to lift the ladder, as it was a necessary object on the path from the chair to the door. And maybe Elli would come back. She should. She said she had no pity. Her father was an invalid. So what? He was not her father. He was a man.

And his thoughts went back to her yellow hair and thin, strong, hairless legs, and small feet in sandals.

He fell asleep on the chair. It was early in the afternoon.

Elli went to see the kids. It was late spring, and the period of "Who is strong?" One of the children had told Gideon where the secret meeting place was—near the spring, above which there was a cave, and as the place was surrounded by reeds and plants it served the purpose.

Elli knew something about the game, but had never seen it played. She knew she had to hide and avoid being noticed.

She approached carefully. She could hear the children's voices. They had gathered not long before. It was the last day of the spring holidays and tomorrow school would begin again.

Elli watched. Rami, Dina's son, was the leader. She used to teach Dina knitting. Rami was Dina's youngest.

Elli's nails dug deep into her hips when she watched, absorbed in the tension and the game. The boys lit a fire and as Rami had a new watch, his first, they timed their resistance to fire.

She wanted to scream—No! and then she was admiring, and then she felt slightly sick to her stomach and couldn't watch, and her thoughts were with Nimrod.

Rami's turn came. The rest of the boys just put a finger in and out. Rami put his whole hand in, watching the watch at the same time.

Elli screamed.

The children rushed toward the sound, where she sat, hiding behind a rock, shaking, her hands covering her face.

"It's Nimrod's girl," Rami said. "Hungarian. I think she's crying," and he said he'd talk to her and make her promise not to tell anybody about the place. He told the boys to go home, and came near her. He couldn't remember her name.

"It's nothing. Look!" he said and showed her his hand. "Just a game. We don't ever burn anything."

Elli was badly shaken. She could smell burning flesh. She could smell her childhood. She could smell and feel the war, and her skin felt as if it was cut and tortured.

"I tell you it's nothing. You shouldn't be afraid. We are all strong and brave and nothing has ever happened."

She couldn't answer. It all came back. Her brother, the World War, the little room she escaped to, the screams, the despair—and the sun of Beit-On and the slow sound of the stream and Rami's confidence couldn't wash it away.

"Are you coming to the village? I'm going down."

She stood up. Everything seemed to be moving in circles, circles of black and white and of burns and small palms, but she took a deep breath and straightened her hair.

"But what for? Why?" she asked Rami, asking the world, asking the village below and the God above. Rami shrugged.

"A game. It's one of our games, like any game. For nothing special. Where are you going?"

"To Gideon's house."

"Well, let's go. It's out, isn't it?"

He stepped on the fire to make sure it was out, and they took the path leading down.

Before they parted Rami made her promise she wouldn't tell anybody. She could tell Nimrod, because he was the Rock, and he was a leader, and Gideon, too, because he was the children's friend, but nobody else.

"Just a game. That's what it is. To play at." And he went away whistling gaily.

She tried to open the door. She did not knock. She just opened the door and noticed that something was blocking it.

"Gideon! It's Elli. Please let me in. I've got to see you. It's for me. Please pity me."

Gideon woke up. Pity me. Someone had said pity me, or was it a part of a dream? He stood up and saw the ladder against the door.

"Anybody there?"

"Yes. Please let me in."

"Well, young lady, this presents some difficulties."

"Stop it, please," she begged, trying to push. "I won't harm you or your noble feelings. You're as cruel as the children. Let me in."

"Hush—sh—sh, don't get excited. The difficulty is purely physical. You'll have to go through the kitchen door at the back. The ladder fell and I can't open the door. On your way you may put the kettle on."

She didn't hear the last part of what he said. She was already hurrying to the back yard, and into the house.

She couldn't talk. What could she tell him? Nothing or everything? Everything? Never. That would mean weeks of self-pity again. That was too easy. That would mean bringing everything up, crying, torturing herself, feeling guilt. So—nothing. But she had to ask, she had to understand or she wouldn't be able to stand it. It was not only Beit-On, it was everything, and Nimrod, and her own children one day.

She started talking to Gideon, fast, confused sentences, Hungarian words patching the gaps.

"Tell me. Explain, please. I saw the game they call 'Who is strong?' They put their hands in the fire. Can someone tell me what for? I don't want to talk about the war. It'll hurt me, and it will hurt you. I had a little brother, like Rami—Dina's son. I've never mentioned it, never will again. I know you're tired of stories of burned children and choked mothers. I know you are building something new and one has to start from scratch and maybe forget everything. I don't say the kids should know about the lives and deaths of kids like my own brother, but why do they play games, why the danger, why the proof? Isn't just being here and living and being free enough proof? Why? What for? No God demands it of his children. They don't prove anything. Why did you send me to see?"

She stopped. She noticed she was crying, and she apologized.

Gideon took her hand in his. He was shivering.

"I'm sorry. I shouldn't have. I could explain, but that would take eternity. What for, you ask. For the hell of it. Your brother wasn't asked whether he wanted to suffer, but the lesson was that we ought to learn to fight back. So we teach the children. They learn faster than they should and they don't even need to fight.

"What's the use of explaining. Look at me. I'm the answer. Stupidity, false courage, something invalid in the road that led to this." He pointed to his amputated leg. "No logic. No wisdom. Not even common sense. Great results, and great danger. And then—it's too late, and a damned ladder falls down and I can't open the door. When I was very young I'd put my hand in the fire to play 'Who is strong?'

"Yes, figure it out. Maybe it'll get into you as well and you won't question it any more. You'll be involved and your own children will be strong and brave and tough and you'll accept it.

"Take care of Nimi. He needs it. Be careful. He's the proudest man ever. Just let him be so. I'm afraid it's too late to change a rock into a breathing plant."

"I love Nimrod," said Elli. "I'm scared. Would you let me come over from time to time?"

"Please do. What happened to the kettle?"

"What kettle?"

Gideon explained.

"I will put some water to boil," said Elli.

They were enjoying the tea and watching the sunset through the open window when Rina entered; Rina, Nimrod's age, used to do the housework at Gideon's. She spoke to him about the farm, brought him papers, and made a meal from time to time. She was the neighbor's daughter and was about to get married to Udi, the son of the village truck driver.

Elli understood Rina even less than she did Nimrod, but almost for the same reasons. Rina was somewhere between two worlds, not a child—she lacked the childish charm and dream quality of the young—and far from being a mature woman. She was good looking and proud, but there was something masculine about her, not bad or ugly, but just a lack of femininity. The way she handled things, her impudence, her anxiety to manage situations and matters. She was good and helpful, and had a certain charm, but the woman in her had died somewhere on the way, when milking the cows, or handling the farm, or wearing slacks. They weren't all like this. Most of the girls in the village were hard workers, but also enjoyed flowers, and ribbons and a warm word. But like Nimrod—well it wasn't quite like that, but there was always something lacking in their path toward being a woman or a man. Rina detested Elli. She thought her a phony. "The delicate plant in Nimrod's garden," she thought. "She could never handle a farm or children," and she suspected Elli would never feel at home. "She is a city girl," she told herself. And now, seeing her with Gideon, her responsibility made her envious.

Elli felt it. She tried to break through but couldn't.

"Are you two talking about dresses?" Rina asked.

"Yes," said Gideon. "I suggested Elli get an evening dress for the harvest party. Have some tea?"

"Oh. So I see I'm superfluous. Your blond friend prepares the meals. Maybe she can also work out the budget problems of your farm and do all my other jobs."

"Don't talk like that. Elli is a friend; what mood are you in anyway?"

"Me? I never have time for moods. Ask Elli about moods. The girls can tell you stories about nights of crying and days of being sulky. She turned to Elli. "How come you are not working today?"

"It's my day off. And I think I'd better go. We have a Hebrew lesson tonight. Shalom."

Elli left.

"If I could get up and slap you, I would," Gideon said to the smiling Rina. "How cruel and jealous can one get?"

"Hell. She is a new immigrant, and so what? It doesn't make them angels. They are people like us, good and bad."

"Yes, only more so. More 'people' than us. Elli went through hell and came back to life, and she is a wonderful woman."

"Woman! Since when do you use terms like this? She is no more woman than we girls, and if being a woman means being frightened at night, and wearing pretty dresses, and keeping your hands delicate and perfumed, I'm not a woman, and I'm glad of it."

"No, Rina, you are not a woman and you never will be. You'll be a good wife and mother, true. You'll cook chickens and potatoes, and bake heavy cakes and make omelets, but you lack the sensitivity and will to understand and to give of yourself. But . . . what right do I have to talk? You are good to me."

"And good enough for Udi. This one"—pointing toward the door, meaning Elli—"will never stay here long enough. Too bad for Nimrod and Ivri, and Miriam. It's strange that Nimrod picked on her."

"She has all it takes, Rina. All that he doesn't have."

Gideon was upset, and his annoyance grew into anger.

He studied Rina, finding all the ugly details in her, her thick ankles, her red hands and uncombed—and burnt at the ends—hair, a stain on her blouse which grew and grew until it looked large and dirty. The new type, thought he, the hair on her legs grew darker and longer. He felt sick.

"Nimrod pities her. That's it. He is devoted and conscientious about the country, so he is anxious not to discriminate and to make the new ones feel at home. It's a sacrifice. He thinks he ought to keep her company. He feels sorry for her."

"You little bitch! Get the hell out of here! How dare you! Go to your Udi and build the land and have half a dozen heroes around you. Go!"

She smiled meekly and left Gideon in the darkened room.

It was late, and it had been a tiring day. Each day was like a bead untied from the others, and he knew they'd scatter one morning and he wouldn't be able to collect them.

The beats of his heart and mind sounded like a blind man's white stick in an eternal darkness, searching, hesitating, moving slowly and aimlessly.

# 14

THE boys of Beit-On weren't automatically drafted into the army, that is to say if there was only one son in the family. These were used to organize the defense system in and around the village, and at the end of the lake —the other side of which was the Syrian border. Nimrod was not to go through the normal phases.

An officer was sent to Beit-On to train and teach the boys, and later a mixed group of youngsters was based just outside Beit-On and was trained with the local men, as a reserve company. Nimrod had a platoon to command and he did it well. It was all a form of training. There was no action yet, but they knew that if anything should happen now in that area, the local boys would do the job and not a regular army company from elsewhere.

It was another drop of preparedness, readiness, another demand which would have to be fulfilled one day and would seek its way out through the burning veins and action-demanding young hearts and bodies.

Among the boys in the auxiliary troop there were two

who became friendly and attached to the local boys—
one because he admired Nimrod, the other because he
admired Rina.

The rest were soldiers, doing their two-and-one-half
years service, obedient, rather bored in their tents near
Beit-On, kept busy by routine duties, kept clean and
shaved trying to impress the three girl soldiers in camp
and their girl friends who'd come to visit on Saturdays,
and waiting, like the rest of the country, for something
to happen and solve it all.

The village carried on—harvest and the chances of rain,
women gossiping at thresholds or in the store, men wearing their best white shirts Friday nights, and families
drinking in the morning papers thirstily. Yoram and Zaki
felt at home, because they were in love.

Yoram loved Rina; this massive figure of hers, and the
direct eyes, the strong hands, and her utter sincerity ap-
pealed to him. She was going to marry Udi, they said. They
said this for many months, and it seemed that Yoram had
no chance.

He was a city boy, clean and neat, somewhat shy but a
good soldier. His father had a factory and he intended to
be in the same business. He found that Rina possessed
all that the city girls lacked, and was charmed. Being fed
up with exhibitionistic, artificial womanhood he saw in
the girl an ideal, the housewife, the mother, the fruitful
creature. Sitting alone on watch he would dress her up, let
her hands rest, tie her hair back, and maybe even add a
dash of lipstick. They'd have many children. He could
afford many, and he'd have the immense pleasure of showing things to her, teaching her, making her discover things
and places, and enjoying the discovery and the surprise.

There was something clean and earthy about her, her thick ankles and her ironed Friday-night shirt.

No one had ever paid so much attention to her, and she was flattered. The flowers every Friday—picked and chosen with love—compliments, a book of poems—its pages marked to draw her attention to a particular line—endearing expressions, all strange, flattering, and appealing to something in her which was not ripe or awake—the woman.

Udi reacted typically. "Who cares! I could buy books if I'd put my heart in it. Let's see him milk a cow! I know Rina better. She is a Beit-On girl, isn't she? Let the fool exhibit his generosity. The company will leave one day and he'll go back to Tel Aviv and his father's factory."

Rina kept everything in her room. She dried the flowers when they perished and kept the books and gifts on a little shelf, and sitting there, knitting a thick sweater for Udi, she thought about the city. It calmed her feelings toward Elli, and she felt she had something in common with Nimrod and wanted to talk to him.

Nimrod laughed. "You and Yoram? And what about Udi?"

"What about him? Just because the village women think of us as a couple and take it for granted, that doesn't mean anything."

"But Yoram will never make a farmer."

"So what? I am not pledged to farming."

He frowned. "You mean leave Beit-On? Home? Leave the lake and King's Forest and your friends? You'll never be able to stand it for more than a day."

"And Elli? Will she be able to stand it here for more than one year, or two, or five?"

"Don't drag her in. That's her problem, not even mine

or yours. She'll manage and I'll help her." Actually it never occurred to him that a Budapest girl wouldn't feel at home and at ease here, at home, for a lifetime. His attitude was —we'll see. That was an easy way out, always, we'll see. Doctor Time. Doctor Minutes and Seconds and Days. Throw the patient to him and let him operate, inject, and cure and decide on the diet. It worked too.

So the women gossiped now about Yoram and Udi and Rina. Another summer approached—dry and hot and hectic. Goats were shot at from the other side of the lake while people were fishing at night, and the atmosphere in the area became hotter. To recompense, to fight back, to teach a lesson were terms used daily. But it was more anger than hatred, more fatigue than tension.

Yoram got command of one of the platoons—the commando boys, the best in the company—and a weekend leave to go to town, see a commander in H.Q., and come back.

Rina decided to go to Tel Aviv with him. She asked Nimrod and Elli to join them, as there was a car going there and back, and they agreed.

They left on a Friday afternoon, in the open command car. Yoram was at the wheel and Rina had put on her best skirt and a clean white shirt, polished her sandals, and happily sat next to him.

Nimrod and Elli sat smiling in the back. At the last minute, when they were ready to go, Zaki was seen running, shouting something in his odd Yemenite accent. He'd got a day's leave. He wanted a lift to Haifa. They were not going to Haifa, they told him. Never mind, he'd go anyway.

Zaki worshiped Nimrod and would do anything for him. He'd watch him like an obedient animal, and would get up and be ready to move whenever Nimrod seemed to want something. For him there was God to whom he prayed everyday behind the tent, and there were the prophets, and there was Nimrod. He loved the superhuman which was almost inhuman in the boy, and the things that Elli feared and admired and kept away from he sucked and swallowed and clung to. Nimrod was flattered and very embarrassed. Little Zaki, short and very dark, ageless, with curly hair and the darkest of eyes, regarded Nimrod as Ivri did, as Elli almost did, and as Lamech and Gideon preferred not to.

He felt inferior and admitted it, admitting with it that he felt fully dependent on Nimrod.

At night, he'd say, "Zaki doesn't want to be alone. Zaki with Commander Nimrod. No problems." This term he learned from Nimrod, who used it often.

He'd say, "Zaki hears BOOM. Zaki runs away. Nimrod hears BOOM, never runs away."

They were enjoying the trip. Rina was puzzled and torn between several emotions, but happy. Elli and Nimrod smiled at each other through the wind, Nimrod explaining the scenery to her, and pointing out places they were passing. Zaki sat, watching Nimrod.

Halfway to Tel Aviv Zaki demanded that they stop. "I want to get off here," he said.

"But this is far from the city. It's just a bunch of villages. You don't know anybody here."

"I want to get out." And he jumped off the car, waved shalom and, smiling, started to walk toward the village.

They all watched him, surprised and worried.

"Let him go," Yoram said. "I know the fellow. He has more brains in his little head than you think. He's too frightened to ever get lost or ever be uncomfortable. On we go."

That night in Tel Aviv Yoram took them to the café

on Dizengoff Street. They'd see the Bohemian life of the city, he said. Quite a change from an evening in the village.

Tel Aviv is a white town, as Jerusalem is gray in the rocks and Haifa green in the lap of the mountain. White squares, large and small, all clean and alive, and the streets filled with people toward the evening. The waiters in the café hurried to return with orders of ice cream, and small cups of coffee.

Nimrod and Elli sat at a corner table, watching. A bearded character talked about beauty, and a tall slim girl, dressed in black, her hair unbrushed, sat listening to him as if he were Moses reappearing. They talked beauty and wisdom and sex and politics—all in abstract terms, sipping cognac from small glasses and using words Elli found difficult to follow. Artists who seldom painted, writers whose last novel had come out ten years before, and journalists who wrote for whoever paid well, laid humanity on the small tables, and, to the neon lights and the sound of other people doing the same, to the sight of hundreds passing on the pavement, they tore it to bits, and patched and fixed and rebuilt it to destroy again.

Yoram said hello to friends and introduced Rina. Rina drank in their words thirstily. She'd never been to this other Israel, where people seemed to live beyond their daily tasks. Not to have to work all the time, or suffer, or be concerned—it was almost like being abroad. Yoram was the object filling the gap between them and her, and she felt she could sit for many evenings, and learn and listen, and maybe one day she'd be able to talk like the tall slim girl and understand the terms the bearded one used. She felt intellectually inferior, like Zaki and Nimrod. She thought Gideon would have enjoyed the evening.

Nimrod had to move toward the corner when a new

group filled the area and demanded space. Two persons
joined him and Elli at the table and ordered drinks.

Elli observed all this sadly. No, it wasn't strange or new.
In the small smoky cafés in Budapest before the war, you
could find groups like this. And in Paris, London, Rome,
and Athens, there were pavements and cafés, people coming to be seen and heard, people drinking from the drug
of intellect for the sake of intellect and losing productivity
as a result, and needing it as a daily meal forever after.
Tongues taking the place of hands, the mind replacing
operations of the mind. This was all so remote, so unbelonging, so unlike the rest of what she knew of the country,
that she felt like a stranger, back in foreign lands among
unknown people.

Nimrod heard the conversation next to him. People dis-
cussed the cruelty of border clashes, demanded peace, coexistence, suggested that immigration be stopped for a
period, or that even some of the refugees be sent back—
words, words, more drinks, more words and words and
words.

"And where are you from?" someone asked him.

"Beit-On."

"Where is that?"

Nimrod got up, took Elli by the hand, and left some
change on the table.

"You don't have to leave just because I don't know where
Beit-On is. I know it exists. Isn't it . . ."

Someone cracked a joke. The group laughed. People
moved along the pavement, young, old, children, women
going home to prepare meals, girls passing slowly, glancing
toward the café, wondering, "Is there anyone here I know?"

"We're going, Yoram."

"Where to?"

"Ask the fellow over there. He'll show you the place on the map. Thanks for the lift. Have fun."

"Hey, wait!" Rina said. "We're just starting! Isn't it a wonderful change after Beit-On? Everything will look so gloomy when we're back tomorrow night."

They didn't hear her. They were both in need of fresh air and took the first street to the right, toward the sea. Freshness came with the light breeze. There was no need to talk. They both missed the lake below and the farmers' greetings during the evening walk.

"You think Rina is truly attracted to Yoram?" Elli asked, anxiously.

"Maybe. I don't know. For a girl it's easier to make the choice. She doesn't have to work, support, or worry, and the city has more to offer her. Yoram is a charming boy. I like him."

"But how could she leave Beit-On?"

"Easily. You saw. Some people don't even know where the bloody place is. Because so much was forced onto her —to be a farmer, to love the cows, to love the village—she now loves to react to it. You can either throw it all behind you, in one blow, or never. If you do it slowly, you'll be tormented and eaten inside until you just fade away— you'll be neither here nor there. I believe you're either born to live in Beit-On or on Dizengoff Street, and as you can't do both you can't really make a wrong choice without it's being noticed." He paused. "So there you are, princess," he said. "Make your choice. I am not going to be another Udi."

She stopped. Her hand left his. Her hazel eyes pierced him in the dark and nailed him to the white wall behind.

"How dare you! Don't you have any self-respect? Aren't you ashamed of yourself? Or is it because you feel something has failed when people like Rina leave, and you want to throw it at me? What do you know about adjustment? When did you have to face a problem? When didn't you have earth and heaven at your feet, first as Nimi, and then the leader and now the Rock? What do you know about loving the soil you take for granted, the sky, freedom, sunsets and sunrises, and the sounds of bells ringing on cattle's necks? How dare you?"

"Still, you have the choice. You haven't explored it all. Beit-On isn't Israel."

"Is the café in Dizengoff? I found what I was looking for—a home, a man I love, hard work, friends, food—things you take for granted. My belief in people returned and I'm able to smile—a smile which you take for granted, yet which I couldn't produce before I met you."

"I'm sorry. I didn't mean to hurt you. I just wanted to see."

"You did. You do all the time. You have to test reactions, make sure, secure yourself so nothing will go wrong. Nimrod, do you love me?"

"Yes, Elli, I suppose I do. I'm not very good at it, am I? Let's walk along the beach. Here, let's get some corn and eat it while we walk."

Eating and munching the corn on the cob she looked fourteen again. Nimrod almost felt good that people didn't know where Beit-On was. It meant it was theirs and it was a very large secret place.

They took off their sandals and followed the stairs leading from the promenade to the sandy beach—to miles of white sand, with the baby waves of summer slow and licking, like bedtime stories, dominating the scene and the night.

An old fisherman was walking along carrying a basket

and he nodded good evening. The sounds of the city became dim and far away and Nimrod's arm was around Elli. He pulled her toward him, and stroking her hair murmured, "Forgive me." He kissed her on her nose, on her ears, on her neck, and, opening his shirt, he drew her nearer and they slowly sank down on the sand, first to sit and then to lie down, he stroking her body, claiming it from the noises and words and smoke of the main street, studying it.

But as before all of a sudden there was only he, Nimrod the man. And as if scared of gentleness he laughed into the air. "I asked it to test you," he said. "I knew you'd be with me and Beit-On, always."

And his firm fingers dug into her hair to untie the ribbon and move along her body and he drank her in, forgetting all.

Very early the next morning they returned to Beit-On.

## 15

THE trip to Tel Aviv upset Nimrod more than he had thought possible. Why, he asked himself, all this tension and worry and involvement if you could sit in a café instead? He didn't speak to Ivri while milking in the morning, and when Ivri asked him, "Is it true we're going to do something about the shooting on the lake?" Nimrod said, "The guys in town want coexistence now. Easy words, as if we want wars."

This was a lie. He did want action, and right then more than ever. Again this double Nimrod was stretched to extremes. He wanted to jump into fire and prove himself and act, or else to fold himself and insert his body back into Miriam's womb or in Elli's arms.

Miriam noticed his mood.

"Is it Elli?"

"No, Miriam. She's a fine girl."

"I'm going to clean your room, young man, and throw half the junk away."

"Go ahead," he said carelessly. He didn't care much for

objects or possessions. They were small souvenirs only, and useless. There was a future, and the present minute and the past were already gone and buried.

I met Zaki in the center. He helped me to carry supplies home. He's sweet, isn't he?"

"Sweet? Yes. Not exactly the new type Ivri likes though. Still, he'll learn. He needs action too."

Nimrod was doing things around the house. It was the end of summer, when the evenings already foretold the fall. A time of death and rebirth for everybody. Nimrod was thinking about possible action. But the nights were too bright now. Things might have to be postponed.

"Nimrod!" His mother looked through the window. "You don't mind if I give the rabbit to Dina's baby, Rami's new brother, do you?"

"Yes, I do. Leave it there." He shivered. The rabbit. How long ago it seemed. Ages and ages. His unsuccessful birthday, the dear rabbit with its button eyes. He should show it to Elli. Maybe even give it to her. She was a child after all. She might go for it.

Unknown warmth filled him when he picked up the animal. His knife was on the same shelf in the cupboard, both untouched. He used a gun now.

"I couldn't shoot and kill my rabbit," he amused himself thinking, "though who knows what Lamech filled it with. I wouldn't be surprised to find a living soul hidden within the hard leather."

The boys used to say that he was as scared as a rabbit. He never was. Maybe he should get Zaki a rabbit. Not this one, another rabbit. But he'd be insulted. Yet he had to learn and strengthen himself. He'd take it to Elli and give it to her. She'd be happy with it, and one day maybe he'd have a child who would like it.

All of a sudden he could play with a toy. It was a moment
—no longer than that—of letting go, of facing something
buried and of the past, of going back beyond the changes
and happenings and streams of ten years. But it could not
last any longer than a moment because the shell had become stronger as it grew inward to kill the soft inside. The
sabra fruit is a warm, large, juicy summer fruit, but it
shrinks in time. It loses both the juice and sweetness, and
the prickly outside. With Nimrod the sharp outside turned
inward to kill and choke and suffocate the sweet, and only
at moments like this—in the late summer, with hot winds
blowing, clouds moving fast overhead, action in the air
and disappointment somewhere—did he touch again the
edge of sensitivity, and the old Nimi came to life in the eyes
staring at the rabbit—only to die again.

"I'll give it to Elli." He wrapped it in an old newspaper
and hurried out to look for her. She was working in the
rose garden behind the school building. Her hair was tied
with a faded blue scarf and she was sweating. A smile wiped
out her fatigue when she saw Nimrod. She almost forgave
him for the doubts and tests on the Tel Aviv waterfront.
He wouldn't do it again.

She took her scarf off and approached him.

"What on earth have you got in the parcel?" She was
curious.

"A rabbit," he said.

"Oh! A live rabbit! Are you going to raise them?"

"It is not a live rabbit. It's a very dead rabbit. Look!"

And the very dead, very old, rather shabby toy was
brought out.

"A toy?" she asked. Her mind worked fast. He was testing her again. He thought her a stupid child. He wanted to
see whether she was a sentimental no-good or a woman,

grown and mature. She was supposed to laugh at toys as he did, to side with him against the trivialties of life, to forget the young childish innocent reactions and be serious and cynical. So she would. She detested the idea of his testing her and examining her reactions, but she had forgiven him already. Besides she knew what was expected of her and planned to live up to it, always, never to fail, to forget the rest, or to somehow dip into it secretly and in the dark.

"Are you having a child that you show me a toy? A rabbit! You should show it to Zaki!"

"I thought you'd like him."

"To look at, yes. He's rather old and shabby. But not to own. I'd like some live ones, or if you want to give me something, I'd like to own a new pair of scissors to cut the roses with. Anyway, you look ludicrous standing with a toy in your hands. The Rock with a rabbit. Here, wrap it up again." She was smiling as she talked and he followed her words and movements intently. She had succeeded, she thought. She rather liked the animal and seemed to remember something he had told her about a birthday gift from Lamech. This must be it then. But she knew she wanted the Nimrod with the knife and gun and fiery eyes and strong hands. The boys she knew in Hungary used to keep their childhood toys, even when they were at universities. Nevertheless she was rather unhappy about the incident and decided to talk about something else.

"Is there going to be any action soon?"

"Not when the nights are bright. We'll go later in the winter I suppose. I must be going now. Forget the rabbit. I just wanted to know if you liked it. We came across it when Mother cleaned the room. She says you should come over soon. Shalom. See you later." He left. The newspaper was torn, and he looked funny—big and handsome and with a package through which the rabbit's ear peeped out.

"So that's it," he thought. "I *am* the Rock, and Elli wants to know if there will be action. I suppose I was a fool to think she'd want a toy. She said once long ago she was a woman. It's like offering the rabbit to Miriam." Maybe he should give the disturbing and useless animal to someone else.

# 16

WHEN he came home he threw it in a corner. It made no noise when it fell. If it were made of glass he'd like to break it, almost as if by mistake. He picked it up and threw it again. Again no noise. It was no use. The eyes looked so human sometimes. He was a fool to think Elli would want it, and a fool to still like it. He picked it up from the floor and put it behind his books in the cupboard, deep in, not to be taken out ever again, he thought, and he turned its head and eyes to the wall.

That same evening he decided to go to the white mountain. He might take Zaki with him. He would see Zaki tonight and talk to him. If not, he'd go alone. It would be even better that way.

Zaki wouldn't even consider it.

"Am I mad?" he asked, "to go across the lines, into enemy land, to climb a mountain. What for?"

"I have enough training to climb and then come down, fast, at night, in danger."

"God help you. But why go?"

Nimrod could never answer this one. Going to the white mountain was all his past and future put together. It was so simple and obvious, and yet he could never explain it to himself. It was a protest and a plea, all the battles he hadn't fought, all the marshes he hadn't help drain, all the acts he wasn't the hero of.

And it was also all the poems he hadn't read, the flowers he hadn't picked, the sky he hadn't hugged, and the fears he had never feared, all in the same stream, pushing and wrestling, wanting to be let free. And this was freedom. To go across, forget countries and borders and politics, to go across because the mountain was white, like in some of Lamech's fairy tales, and clean and pure, and so near some days you could almost touch it. He didn't ask why or try to explain. He was going to leave the next evening for the white mountain and climb to the snowy cap, touch it and come back, and it was like going to touch the sky and picking a star, or touching the very heart of his own God who left the pink house many years ago to settle in grains of soil and branches of trees and heaps of hay and heights of mountains.

He made Zaki promise and vow and swear he wouldn't tell anybody. Zaki didn't suspect the extreme danger and the possible death. His admiration of Nimrod was stronger, and if Nimrod chose to do it, he must have his reasons and they were sound and sensible. As for him, as long as he had the choice, and Nimrod didn't at all insist, he would cross no border, nor come near it. It was one more thing where he felt Nimrod was not only superior but incomprehensible as well, and he let it go at that.

"When will you be back?"

"Sometime, in two days or so."

"See you then. God be with you. It must be cold now

up there at night. Take a pull-over. Going to tell Elli?"

"Going to tell nobody."

Zaki was very happy about this. Nimrod the Rock trusted in him only. He wouldn't tell anybody but him—Zaki the Yemenite. It added a great deal to his self-importance and he was grateful.

"Taking a gun?"

"No, what for? It's too heavy to carry, and if I'm caught, I'd better be caught without a weapon. Might take a knife to peel oranges with," he smiled. "Be good. I'll be back soon."

They shook hands; Zaki's was sweating.

It is very difficult to analyze the deed, to know how much of it was a result of youthful stupidity, what part the physical attraction of the mountain and snow played in it, what part looking for danger. Or perhaps it was an unconscious will to encounter fear, an element within him stronger than himself. Or was it to rediscover Lamech's God? Or to show off and establish his reputation as the Rock? Or perhaps it was a lack of confidence, a wanting to show off to himself, to live up to a standard set for him by his parents, his village, his people, and later himself.

Judging from Nimrod's diary it was a very simple operation. Written in a rather childish manner, containing many descriptive details which are omitted here, this is Nimrod's account of the trip, as he saw it.


*Friday morning, September*

Tonight I'll climb Mt. Chermon. I have never felt the touch of snow and the white cap is very inviting. I told Zaki about it, but couldn't tell Elli or Gideon, as they are likely to get scared and try to prevent me from going. It must be beautiful to approach the snow early in the morning.

I have good maps of the area, and if I walk about three miles every hour I can make it in ten hours at the most from the border. I'll have to sleep the day on the slope coming down and return Saturday night. Sunday morning we have training, and I'll have to be present.

I will try to take as little as I can in the way of equipment—warm clothes, food for three days, which is more than I really need, the maps, and my small knife just in case. . . . But of course I won't use it. I don't deem it necessary to take my weapon as I am going on a sight-seeing trip, to climb the Chermon, and not to spy on anybody or clash with an enemy.

I told Yoram I was going to the farm, and Ivri and Miriam think the army unit has sent me to a meeting in Haifa, so there is only a slight chance of discovery if I'm careful enough.

I realize now how badly I always wanted to go to the Chermon, as much now as wanting Elli, or wanting a son or loving Beit-On. I am rather glad Zaki refused to go, which means I can have it all for myself. To love it, to hug it, to drink in the view and absorb the experience—like eating a sweet cake all by myself, or an important day. And the day is important.

I packed all the things I'll take in a small bag, and I will change into an Arab costume near the border, where I'll darken the color of my skin as we're likely to get another bright night.

There are a few small villages on the way, but taking the valley of the river Banias, and not the Hasbani or the

Jordan will help me to avoid populated areas. The branch of the river leads in a wadi to Burj El Bark at 3,900 feet and from there on a steep climb of 5,000 to Kasr Antar —the summit. I will be moving along the Lebanese-Syrian border, but it makes no difference as they are both enemy lands and I have to avoid people. True, I know very little about the conditions, army units, or camps, not much more than the map can tell me, but as I'm going to reach the summit, whatever happens, I'll have to be careful and learn while I move along.

I am so happy because I will be throwing behind all the daily worries, the pettiness, the small intrigues of people unhappy with themselves, and indulging in the world, a big world which gains meaning opposite the mountain.

True, it seems so simple from here but I hope it won't be. Not a fight. I'm not looking for one, but something to overcome, a challenge. Since I used to play games with the kids ten years ago I haven't really had to overcome anything, within me or my surroundings. As I haven't yet started I shouldn't really write, so farewell Beit-On. Your son goes to rape the virgin whiteness.


*On the border, Friday, early evening*
I am all ready, stretched like a spring ready to snap. I have to await darkness, another hour or two.

It's rather cool because of the river, and a certain mist hovers over the valley. I can see clearly the other side and can plan the first part of the way. At moments I am excited, and then the trip is like an imaginary walk to King's Forest. I am going to pick some snow from the Chermon, like flowers for Elli or hay from the top of the stack.

Three countries meet here—Syria, Lebanon, and mine. At this time of evening borders mean so little. The beams of the setting sun don't stop at the border stone and the cool air continues to flow above the border area that is mined, and on both sides you can hear shepherds hurrying to collect their flocks to go home.

Damn, I'm no pacifist. Neither do I care for war. I can't adjust to the idea that this is my enemy. Maybe because he's too close, feasible, touchable, and peaceful.

If I could avoid seeing him, and instead imagine him as a living monster, maybe I could hate him, clash and struggle with him. But I can't this way. I'm going over because he owns a beautiful object which I want to touch and stroke.

True, it's an adventure and fun and exciting, but it's not only that.

This is the river I'm to follow, the Banias. Here it joins another forming a pool and splashing and roaring they descend together, collecting into one river—the Jordan.

I touch the water. This is what happens to the snow on top. It runs downhill into the stream, the wadi, and we use the white majestic purity to irrigate corn with, and the large dirty tongues of cows lick it and roots of weeds struggle to get to it, but at the beginning it's untouched, and that's what I want to touch, lick, let irrigate me. There used to be a Roman road here. There was a Roman town nearby. Before the Romans were the Greeks, the Persians, the Assyrians, the Babylonians, the kings, the judges, the Hittites, the tribes. After the Romans were the Arabs, the Crusaders, the Turks, the British—and it is me, Nimrod of Beit-On, son of Miriam and Ivri, who is here now.

God, all that long history does make me feel small, a

link, who knows maybe only a patch—or maybe a new chain.

I can see the hills from here, low and bare and changing into higher hills and then mountains, their slopes cut and wrinkled by an endless number of wadis, not too steep, just huge and comfortable.

I'm all dressed for the way—the Arab headwear, my face dyed with mud, a large robe hiding my bag, boots, a light wooden cane I keep carving with my sharpened knife. Could they see me now at home they'd think I was playing games. I wonder if Ivri ever had the desire to climb this one. He couldn't have because he would have climbed it before the war started. Well, he did enough as his share, marches and rough land and then drought and heat in Beit-On, so now it's my turn and I'm lucky to climb the Chermon.

It is dark now and I can't write too well. I should avoid being noticed by light or matches. I sit in the reeds and listen to the water. There are evening mosquitoes and dogs barking in the distance—I should beware of dogs, they are a danger around the villages. Time to go.


*Saturday, 1 a.m.*

It's cooler than I thought it would be, but the thick pull-over Miriam knitted is too hot, heavy, and uncomfortable. I'm halfway up. So much seems to have happened, but on the whole nothing really, as I'm here.

Crossing was easy. I took the risk and walked through an area marked Mines. I heard the boys once say it wasn't really mined, and I'll never know. I'll return through the same pass tomorrow night.

The first two hours were tricky—people, dogs, houses—but now in the hills and the lower part of the mountain it's very quiet and deserted.

I met an old man crossing one of the dirt roads. He waved to me and I greeted him back in Arabic, which comes in handy. He asked me, "Where from and where to?" I answered the names of two villages marked on the map. I felt so sure and secure I could almost say, "From Beit-On to the Chermon," but why take risks and play games, or is it all a game?

The air is very fresh here. Up to this point I followed a wadi. Now I will just walk up, moderately, until the morning, when I hope to arrive.

I am hungry. It is good to have the thick sandwich Miriam prepared. If she only knew where it was to be eaten, 4,000 feet above the sea, 4,500 feet above our lake, high above the Azmon.

So clearly I remember, clearer than many childhood memories, climbing the Azmon with Ivri—it was just "Father" then, and Gideon, when he could walk. I hated it then at moments, but I was so proud. Don't I actually hate it now? What am I doing it for? That's what Elli would ask. She'll never know. Maybe one day I'll let her read these lines. Whenever I look at Gideon I remember climbing the Azmon, him running forward, mocking, teasing, poor thing. He would have liked it here.

Nobody around. Wide distances kissing the horizon. It is a bright night. I can stand up and spread my arms and be blessed by God and I am alone. Ivri said once not to trust people and avoid many friends. How good and simple it is to be alone. I'd like my son to climb here alone one day, and drink the hot coffee from the thermos and eat thick sandwiches and conquer nature. Not really. It over-comes me, but by letting go, by giving myself to it, giving my soul as a contribution and my body as a sacrifice I am the conqueror.

My feet are frozen through. I am wearing two pairs of socks. I'd better move on. I remember when I was climb-ing the Azmon I wouldn't stop to think or look. I had to hurry to reach the top. I should do so now.

Elli is asleep. Yoram, Rina, little Rami, Gideon—tossing in his bed. Ivri dreaming—he always dreams. The whole cosmos is asleep. There is nobody, absolutely nobody, who is climbing Mt. Chermon right now but me. Nimrod, alone in the world. I have to continue now to make the summit before dawn.

*Saturday, 5 a.m., summit of Mt. Chermon*

I still can't believe it. Right at this moment I can watch the sun rise, and I am touching snow. Mother, Father, Elli, Gideon, and Zaki can you see me here? I am the black spot in the center of the white snow. I am the beating heart in the middle of the dead cold white desert. I am the tired, living, feeling being on the top of nowhere. I am the human, mortal inferior man. Hear me, Elli? I am man, near to God. I know it's boasting and bragging, but I'm here. Nimrod. They called me girlish names when I was young because my hair was curly. In Haifa I once pushed a little boy under a car, and I cried bitterly when Lamech died, and could tell nobody about it. I made love to Elli in the forest and—and—and— This is me. Here. There is no logic, no purpose, no result or reason, I know, but joy, clarity, cleanliness, aloneness. The snow is death, godly death. The white is a dead color and I miss the greens, but how alive will the green be now that I've conquered the white! No house, building, or even a ruin. I lost my way twice coming up. I arrived at the wrong summit and had to descend and climb again. I couldn't walk on the snow but it's from last year and there are many dry patches in between and I managed, and there is my sun, struggling through the mountains around to throw blazing intoxicating beams out, the wet reflecting substance of snow around me. "Who is strong?" I shout. You know where the echoes come from this time? From the Jordan and the Litani below, from the road to Damascus on the north, and from the low ceiling of the sky. I am the leader, and I ask who is strong. Nimrod gets up and says he's strong. He is small and shy and wants to do something tough, to run under a car, to climb the highest tree in the valley, to swim in the deepest water, and I ask him, "Show me you are strong." He says he'll climb the Chermon. He says he'll climb as nobody ever did. He says he'll lose his way and find it again and be cold and hungry and tired to his bones, and the blood in his veins will want to cease moving. He says he'll touch the snow and bring its feeling to Elli. And he says he'll climb up to God because Lamech used to say we very often climb down to a ladderless well.

And he did. I stand up and I look at Nimrod and I know he deserves to be the leader. As Ivri dried the marshes and Gideon fought the wars, he climbed Mt. Chermon, the mountain of snow as the Arabs call it. Gebel Eth-Thelj.

It was hard. I feel free writing like this, knowing I'll show it to no one. The difficulty now will be coming back, carrying with me as a precious pearl this bit of life, as a beam of sun or a glance at the other side of the moon. In the distance I can see my country. I wave good morning to it, and I'll have to look for a shelter for the day, and rest and sleep and then go back down. Sunday is a normal day and we have to do some training. No night can ever be as complete as tonight. This is my mountain now, a conquered friend.


*Saturday, 12 noon—at 6,000 feet*

On Saturday God rested, and today Ivri put on his white shirt. A few old men will go to the pink house and I have to spend the day waiting.

Never before have I gone through this kind of waiting. From sunrise to sunset, to wait slowly for the sun to disappear, for the shadows to become long, longer, longest— till they are sunken in black—to sit and do nothing but count the minutes, watch around and let my mind pierce the walls of the heart to rediscover what's hidden in there.

Looking for a place wasn't easy in these bare hills and curving wadis, but I'm now in a deserted house, not far from a village. It is some type of shelter, and I'm lucky as it looks as if it might rain. It'll be the first rain. Maybe I brought it with me from the Chermon.

I had an odd experience earlier this morning. When I arrived in the ruin, I fell asleep, almost immediately. I woke up around eleven hearing, or at least I thought I heard, steps. I reached for the knife, and holding it tight crawled on all fours to the small window and looked out. A man had his back turned to me; a very old-fashioned rifle was hung clumsily on his shoulder and he was looking around. He was dressed in a dirty black abaya and white headwear. I was thinking about the gun. Could he shoot, would he shoot if he saw me? I was dressed only in the pullover and slacks and sandals, and looked everything but a

local Arab. My hand was holding the knife. The easiest
thing was to attack him from the back with the knife and
end him this way. It would not be a fair fight, but if he
discovered me it would be the end of many things. I looked
again at the knife. Yes, it was long and sharp enough, but
somehow I didn't feel my life was endangered, and had no
desire to get up, move, crawl, and tear the black cloth from
the back and the ribs of this old man. Still, if he noticed
me, I was lost. I have never killed a person. All of a sudden
I remembered Naifa, the old Arab woman I knew. She
sold watermelons. Maybe she was now in his village or
maybe she was dead. I knew her many years ago. This old
man wasn't an enemy, he was an old man who meant nothing at all to me. I couldn't care less if he was dead or alive
or happy or miserable. My hand didn't sweat or tremble,
and my body was erect and ready. If he turned, if he approached the ruin, I'd have to kill him. I would have to
kill. It was very simple. And all of a sudden it mattered
not at all. It wasn't even like climbing the mountain or
the tree. I would sit, I thought then, and once he was near
enough I would have to kill him.

He did come nearer. I was thinking about the clouds and
the rain and Elli at home. If we were in action, I'd have
shot him without hesitation. As it was now, it would be just
killing because I had to, for myself, not for the country,
not revenge, not courage, just killing—like killing a snake
ready to coil around you or like killing Naifa, almost. Soon
it would be winter, and there would be rain and more snow
at the summit, but now it was the old Arab opposite me.
He came nearer, looked around, and abruptly turned to go
away. I watched his slightly bent back, and pushed the
knife back into the bag. I still had some food and prepared

my lunch. I have a few hours now before darkness, and will try to sleep.


*Back home, Sunday morning*

I told Miriam I'm writing a report. I told her I'm tired and feel fine, and I put the contents of my bag back in place. When I put the knife away it was odd to think that it could have been used. If Zaki had been with me, I'm sure I would have killed the Arab. But I don't know. . . .

The way down was the easiest part. I almost walked straight back, like going home from the center of the village, back through a different way, along the Jordan, crossing at the same point, through the mine field. Never, never will I know whether there was any danger involved. Was I merely lucky or was I smart enough or was I close to death? After crossing I went to the main road and got the very early bus toward the lake of Kinereth, and then walked the few miles into Beit-On.

I am tired and satisfied. I suppose people who are drunk feel like that the morning after. I have a hangover of sorts but the picture is not clear. I have mixed images and re-actions and above all I see the black spot in the center of the white vast area of snow. And this was me.

I can see the Chermon from here. It's like a battle which is done with and sealed forever. I did my part and now there is peace. I'm at peace with the mountain and nature and myself because I overcame them all. Now I deserve the title of Rock, like Gideon or the others, and feel more free than ever before. On the way I thought about Elli. I know I'm very young, but as I'm sure I'll never feel this way about anybody else, I do want her to be my wife. I know I can't offer her much—my farm, my work, loyalty, strong hands, and some attention. Perhaps she'll settle for these. She is my first woman and I want no second or third.

It's a pleasure now to look at the mountain, for we share a big secret. It's as if it was doing me harm by lying there untouched, but spread out and noticed and wanted, and I took action. And it's a bill settled now, because the mountain accepted my challenge.

How silly borders can be, if you can cross them and come back and still maintain war. But this trip was above and beyond the war, the situation, the state. It was a trip into manhood, a wish fulfillment in its utter and complete sense. It was living a white dream, every moment of it.

I will get a couple of hours sleep. Miriam is heating some water for me. I do just about need a shave, and can't wait to see Elli. I can't tell her about the gift, but I brought her back a gift—flowers from the slopes of the Chermon, and myself as a man.

Nimrod finished writing, shaved, took a shower, and slept for a couple of hours. The word "fear" was never mentioned in his notes. He knew it not, like a child whose senses aren't yet operating, the way some are dumb and some are deaf. He knew it not. When he woke up he took the bunch of flowers and put on clean clothes. He was going to deliver his gift to his woman. The Chermon smiled.

## 17

THEY started building behind the house. Nimrod thought it would be better to add another story to the house but Elli preferred a separate building at the back.

She accepted the idea of getting married that fall without questioning the time, reason, or manner. The atmosphere in the village had invaded her. It was normal to want to get married as soon as you thought you had found the right person, to conceive and give birth, to take over the farm and carry on. And as Beit-On had become her home, and she did love Nimrod, there was no reason to wait any longer.

Rina gave Yoram the sweater she had knitted for Udi. Like many of the things she did, it was an unfair though sincere act, and was accepted as such. Udi never complained. He grew sad and remote for a while and then started looking around and was seen more and more often with Anat.

So even the gossiping women in Beit-On were not surprised when Rina announced she was going to marry Yoram, and that they would get married at the same time as Nimrod and Elli and give the whole village a reason to celebrate.

And then Nimrod made a mistake. He suggested that the wedding take place at Gideon's house and not in his own, as Ivri didn't mind. But Gideon's agreement had to be obtained.

"I'm getting married," Nimrod stated.

"Yes, Rina told me. I thought you would. What's the hurry?"

"Why wait? Who knows what the morrow brings and we'll be very happy now."

"Did you ever think about why you're getting married?"

"Why? I love Elli."

"Poor girl, a nice one too."

"What do you mean, 'poor girl'? She's happy."

"Yes, but for how long? How long will it be before you turn into the way I was, and then there will be only you around? How long before you'll start taking her love and being for granted and stop kissing her at night? How long before she'll become only a part of the farm?"

"Never. She's equal to me, and I don't see why you talk like this."

"I don't mean to hurt you. It's but a warning. Please be good to her. She went through more than we all realize and wounds of the heart take long to heal. So be good to her, remember she is there, try to give of yourself, even though you're not made to give."

"Look, Gideon. I came here to ask you if we could get married on the lawn in front of your house. I thought you'd like that."

Gideon grew very suspicious. He rose from his seat and stared at the young man.

"Go now. Don't come back until you find other feelings

in you than pity and hatred, or indifference. Go away and
wander around and seek love, understanding, fear, laughter,
and get rid of those who condescend. Throw your pity to
the dogs who like it, or pad the mattresses of the poor ones
with it, but don't waste any on me. What a hilarious joke!
Celebrate here! So that poor Gideon who can't move will
at least be able to see. See what? See destruction, or happiness or love? You know how I longed for a son once? You
know how long it has been since I touched a woman? And
I wasn't wounded down there," he said, pointing to his
organs, "or up here in the heart, not really.

"Oh, I talk too much again. Go away, Nimi. I'm sorry.
You know I love you and hope you'll be the happiest man
on earth. Now go and get married, in your own house.
Make Ivri and Miriam happy, and maybe we can arrange
for me to come. I can make it to the gate now!"

"Shalom," Nimrod said, departing. "I don't know why
but you make me sad by talking like this. More than that.
You know you are wrong. I suppose bitterness should be
let out on the best friends we have and I don't mind. Take
care of yourself, friend. Elli sends her love. So does Rina.
See you soon."

Ivri thought he should talk to Elli before the wedding.
He went to the school to look for her and didn't know how
to start talking or what exactly he had in mind. Elli was
like a flower and Ivri didn't care much for flowers, he was
even rather afraid of them.

"Shalom, Ivri. How are things at home?" Elli surprised
him by coming up from behind.

"Shalom. Everything's fine. I passed by and thought we'd
chat for a moment. So, you're happy aren't you?"

"But of course. I love Nimrod, and you and Miriam, and
we'll have a home at last."

"You know Nimrod is difficult, tough and rough at times, and he's very devoted to the country and places it above everything else. I hope it won't hurt you ever. He's just made this way."

"I know. I think I can share it with him. You shouldn't worry."

"You don't have any family left, do you?"

She pondered sadly, pictures flying through her mind getting nowhere.

"I don't know. This is awful but I just don't know. I know my mother and brother died, but my father just disappeared. We escaped after they were killed and we never met or heard about each other since. He doesn't know I'm alive. Maybe we'll never meet again. I read about families reunited after searches and I am filled with hope, but how? Maybe he's in Tel Aviv, or in Rio, or in Budapest. He's probably changed his name, and he doesn't look for me because he thinks I'm dead. If he could only be here to see me and Nimrod happy. When we parted he said that one day he'd come to greet his grandchildren somewhere. I think he's dead."

"I'm sorry. Anyway, you have a home now, and you are like our daughter. You understand that living on the farm presents certain responsibilities but I'm sure you can meet them and get along well with Miriam. We both feel that we are taking part in helping to build one people when our son marries an immigrant."

"Don't talk like this! Your son marries the woman he loves. It has nothing to do with 'one people' or integration. I am not a part of a five-year plan, and there is no sacrifice involved." She touched Ivri's arm. "I don't mean to be rude, but you can relax and think of yourself as you are, your son as a man and person, and Miriam as a mother.

And you can think of me as a loving woman. Not everything is tied in with the massive past struggle and achievement, please."

He left without thinking. As usual, when there was a
problem like this, he'd wave it aside and try to forget it,
push it underground, dust it into fresh air and carry on.

It was a big wedding. Yoram's family arrived from Tel
Aviv, and the whole village was there. Everybody said,
"Aren't they lovely?" and Miriam cried and said she was
happy. The rabbi conducted the ceremony and they drank
sweet red wine from tiny glasses lent by the big village
store for the occasion.

The girls admired Elli's simple dress, white and short
and pleated, and the men went through the routine jokes
about marriage, first nights, and freedom.

The two couples hardly had time to think or sense the
occasion. They were in the center as objects, a reason to be
happy, drink wine, or tell jokes, and afterward the morrow
would be just another day for the rest.

Elli disappeared. Nobody noticed it and she was hurrying down the road toward Gideon's house when she stopped
halfway.

"Why, Gideon, how come you're here?"

"The bride! The beauty! I decided to come, but halfway
is right for me. That's exactly where I stand. Between the
house and the dust, between aloneness and the human
sounds of happy people, between the dark and the light,
or life and death. Damn it, no philosophy. I just can't make
it. I can't make anything. I feel like cursing. You're the
wrong company for that. Will you help me home?"

"No, you must come, Nimrod will be very sad, and Rina,
and Yoram, and of course myself."

"Cut it out! Look, there is no way out of my situation.

It's getting worse and I hate it even more because it makes me bitter and selfish and hating. So keep out of my way, and remember I care for you very much. Think of me as dead, I beg you. Pray for my soul to find peace. Name your son **Gideon** if you wish, just as if I were dead, and be happy.

"I feel filthy, the dirt of the race. I feel like blaming and yelling at people, and you're so clean and wonderful and it is your happy day. Shalom. Good luck. I have a wedding gift for you. Here. And now I have to go."

Elli opened the parcel as Gideon slowly made his way from her. In childish clean handwriting there were all his poems copied and neatly arranged in a notebook. It was dedicated to her. It said, "The little cleanliness in me is all there, and it's yours." Elli returned to the party, hid the notebook in her bag, and joined the rest.

"Here is my wife!" Nimrod shouted and lifted her up. He never noticed the tear in her eye when they started dancing the Horah, a sweeping and bowing dance, feet and hands and hair and eyes as if burned in fire or motivated by passion. All seemed to go around in larger and larger circles opposite her eyes, dancing and crying and sweating, and spots and circles growing larger—covering all—and shrinking again and larger again, until the early hours of morning.

## 18

THE cottage was completed and Elli and Nimrod moved in. Elli didn't have many things of her own, and a trip to Haifa to the village's co-operative furniture shop did the rest. In the beginning of the winter Elli became pregnant and the rumors about "taking action" were turned into a secret plan, and people were waiting for a dark night.

The fact that Nimrod now was married and his wife was expecting didn't prevent him from waiting for a battle and preparing for it. He would come home, change his shirt, lie on his bed in the twin-bed bedroom, and look at the ceiling.

"I'd give all I have to do something serious."

Elli would come and sit and listen to him. She was used to it by now.

"I just don't see why we're waiting. They shot at the boats once again. I'm fed up with the talks, and guesses and training. The company is rotting and getting stale and life feels empty. It's the tension I can't stand. You understand?"

"Yes. I suppose so."

"Yoram is a coward, I think. Or at least he doesn't care. Just because Rina is pregnant he leaves weekends and goes home to her. He is happy and content. God, I hope whatever you carry in you will have a better time than I."

She came nearer and tried to stroke his hair. He pushed her aside.

"You'd like the bullets to do it instead of me," she said almost to herself. "We are just married, and I have forgotten what the taste of your lips is. You'd give all you have to let go and relax afterward. Me and the child too?"

She was sad, felt and looked sad, and grew lonely and almost wished for a battle as strongly as Nimrod did, as she thought this might change him.

One evening he came home and kissed her but didn't change his clothes. "Tonight! We're off tonight. We're a part of a large operation across the border. Syria. The same village that attacked the fisherman. Here! I knew they'd do it at last. We're not alone in it but we will be the first ones to cross and open fire while the other troops will move along to attack from the rear." He kissed her again and lifted her up. "You're getting heavy, woman! Don't forget to tell your baby that when it was two months inside you his father won a battle.

"Now! Some food, my battle outfit, my knife, boots, a kiss for good luck, and I'm off!"

Elli had awaited this moment in horror for months. Gideon had told her his own war experiences and how he was wounded. She wanted to talk to Nimrod, to tell him to realize the danger, to fear the unknown and take care, but she never could and maybe never would—

Silent and sad she left the room. Each piece of bread she cut hurt her, and each egg she broke and fried broke something in her.

"Some coffee!" Nimrod shouted. "Black, please."

She obeyed quietly and wished the pulse of the world would stop beating right that minute. "Let us all freeze and be tied and nailed," she thought. "Let me never leave the kitchen, let Nimrod never leave this house or my child the womb, as what is it all for?" His eyes were shining in a way she had never seen before and the pride in his face was not pleasant to see. She knew he didn't love war or shooting or killing, and she couldn't understand or ask him why he did this.

Before he left she asked him, "Will you kill people?"

"Here, we have a pacifist at home. I don't want to, if that is what you ask, but this is not the question. I have to do a job, and do it well, and it's important that I do so. Shalom, Elli. Take care. I won't be long. Sometime in the morning I would love a hot shower."

"Does Ivri know? And Miriam?"

"Yes. They didn't make such a fuss. They knew I'd go one day. Miriam was a bit upset, I think, so you females can spend the evening together. But go to sleep early. The doctor said you needed it. Don't think of me. I'll just go and come back."

"Are Zaki and Yoram going along?"

"Sure. It'll be very important for Zaki."

She noticed him frown and think for a second. She came nearer.

"You are not afraid, Nimrod, are you?"

"Never." He laughed harsh, unpleasant laughter, and waving good-by left.

She could hear the echo of his footsteps long after he was gone, for many, many hours.

Silence echoed from the mountains. The men were walking well spaced apart, wrapped in their own worlds of thoughts and feelings. Zaki didn't keep the space and moved toward Nimrod, almost touching him. In the eyes of the men you could learn of droughts, a sick mother left at home, half a bottle of cognac left behind, children kissed good night, blood, excitement. In Zaki's eyes you could learn paralyzing fear, and in Nimrod's complete peace, as if paradise was just there, in the Arab village on the hill, and it wasn't the blood or the killing or hope that you could see. It was all there, like a first love affair.

It was too dark to notice the scenery, but one could smell the odor of flowers, wet grass, men's sweat, and near Zaki the smell of fear, the physical overwhelming smell of fear.

Nimrod was thinking of nothing. He was one of those cases when the body operates, the legs carry the body on rhythmically, and the machine up in the head stops ticking; when one indulges in luxurious being without thinking.

And the first shot was heard, screaming like a pain shot into the flesh of night and trees and barking dogs.

The barks were in answer to the shot, not aggressive, attacking barks but an echo to the sound of the bullet whispering in one's ear.

The next moment was the one Nimrod delighted in. The one moment, a long one, of awaiting the answer. They had sent a message which was fast and deadly and—Who? Where from? How would they be answered? It could come from anywhere, and everywhere, or worse—never come. Lips tried to smile. Yoram said good night and shut his eyes. Zaki's eyes were searching around as if trying to figure out how to get away. They were very near the village and its police station. Some cries were heard. Lights were turned on and off again, and then the answer came. Veins constricted for a minute into blue marks on the skin. Nimrod smiled, not a malicious smile, almost as if forgiving their hesitance. The first shot was heard. They had to wait for the attack from the rear and then move in.

"Fire!" Kickbacks of the gun. They had to attract the enemy's attention. Automatic movements, more sweat, and a holy silence.

It wasn't a battle really, as it wasn't a war. Nor was it a game, not when you heard the poisonous shrieking of the bullets—confused, scattered, searching above your heads— there were no feelings of deep revenge or hatred. It was almost as quiet as a day's work, only moments seemed eternal and seconds endless.

And all of a sudden time and morale and sense and silence were all lost, drowned in the whirlpool of battle. Orders were shouted and obeyed, men came running to the attack, into the station, throughout the village across narrow streets, between fences. Warm hands were holding guns, shoulders were already immune, eyes burning, and the darkness which promises everything and denies all— behind the wall, across the road, on top of the roof there could be an enemy, or one of the boys, or a dead figure, a pool of blood, a pair of child's shoes, your own image in a window, a bush in blossom. Not a war, or a battle, but a fight.

Nimrod's operation was cold and confident. There was not a moment of hesitation, wildness, or horror. He moved like a tiger, cleaning and clearing his way, never looking back or behind, when Yoram called him.

"Well, fighter, doing well! Listen, take four boys and move along the forest. You are to plant this bomb under the railway bridge and be back in time for us all to clear out before the auxiliary forces arrive. Don't shoot on the way. Be fast and whatever happens don't let it stop any of you from coming back as you'll be holding up the company awaiting your return. Can you make it?"

"You've said it. I won't be long!"

Nimrod selected three boys and was ready to move when he noticed Zaki. It was one of those moments of silence within silence, when the earth comes to a stop, and you can hear the elongated echo of the last shot before the next one follows and you all stop in tension, feeling like yelling into the air or opening fire at the next trunk or burying your head in the soil, and Zaki begged with his dark black pools of eyes not to be separated from Nimrod.

"Come along boy. We're going for a walk."

Zaki followed, last. They walked well spaced apart, hiding in the shadows of trees, listening carefully to the shots—they advanced, marking the end of the battle like the last few drops from a tap after you've shut it.

There was the bridge, the rails, the bomb placed by Nimrod quickly and neatly, a match and then back, fast. The company was waiting. The fire opened and the distant heavy elephantlike noise of trucks and tanks was heard clearly. The aid was arriving.

The four men were discovered. The early light of dawn revealed indistinct shapes and figures and colors. The company was waiting, hurry. Zaki was first now, Nimrod last.

It felt like a stroke, almost a warm one, and the pain came after—a wound in the arm.

Nimrod paused for a moment. The three hurried toward him.

"It's nothing, march on. Just a scratch. A bad job at that." He looked at his own flesh while walking on. The wound was bleeding. It was the first time he saw his own blood, red, juicy, very warm and flowing, and the pain, changing from a short electric pain into a hammering one and then a sharp pain with every step.

"It's strange," he thought, "the blood feels good on the arm." It was almost like a contribution to something important, a hymn with every step, of pride and pain and manhood, a hymn to his body again.

He wasn't sick or disgusted with his own blood. It was a new sensation. He touched it when changing a handkerchief, and it felt detached, as if his hand were a patient in a clinic. And yet the pain was there and he did his job. They were under fire now. They could see the trucks silhouetted, pulling small cannons behind, and they had to hurry. There was a cultivated field to cross between the forest and the station where the company waited. They'd have to crawl and run.

Nimrod talked fast. "Listen, boys. I'll open machine-gun fire and cross the field nearer to them," he said, pointing to the direction of the shots. "Meanwhile, you hurry fast, but fast, across, as low as you can. Crawl, lie down, get up and run, and throw yourself again behind any possible shelter. It's a short run and we can make it. Don't wait for me.

"If one of you is wounded, try and take him along. If that's impossible, leave him and carry on. We have no time to lose. On. Act!"

The men started moving. Nimrod watched them for a second and turned his machine gun toward the forest. He opened fire and started moving while shooting when he saw Zaki bend and fall in the middle of the field. The other men instinctively rushed back toward him. The fire was concentrated now around the four, a heap of human living flesh as clear as a target in full daylight.

Nimrod shouted, "Keep running. Leave him. I'll take him."

They hesitated and then separated and moved on.

Nimrod was very near to Zaki; he could hear his heavy breathing and moaning. He was crying "Mother" and "God," and whenever the pain was strong he screamed "Nimrod!" Nimrod was lying now next to him. They had a few moments before the sun would be up, and the company just *had* to start moving. Zaki looked ugly. He was wounded in the stomach and all Nimrod could do was put the large field bandage on top to prevent dirt, and maybe to stop the bleeding for a while. The white around the black pupils of Zaki's eyes looked sick and desperate and he was a heap of blood and dirt and sorrow. Nimrod tried to pull him along, but Zaki screamed, and he bent above him, so near as to smell the stomach and blood. "Listen, boy. I'll have to leave you. Don't be afraid. They won't kill you. They know you are wounded. They'll take you and then return you. I hate to do it but there is no choice. We're holding the company up and there is nothing I can do. If I stay here they'll go on shooting at me and we'll both end this way. So just don't move. Don't think, don't fear, and wait."

He didn't wait for an answer. He knew he was right and obeying orders, and he moved on. He could hear Zaki behind him crying, "Nimrod don't leave me! I don't want to be alone! Nimrod, I'm scared! Scared! Scared!"

His scream went high into the sky to meet the rising

sun when Nimrod reached the station and reported to Yoram.

The company had to move, and hurrying they left toward the bushy slopes, the place where the river joins the lake, and went across the border.

They didn't leave a whole night behind. They left many moments, the moments of action, and the ones in between. Now there was anxiety and joy, and just tired unshaved faces, red eyes, weary heavy bodies, dirt, and slow conversation.

On the truck Yoram counted the losses. It was a successful operation, the police station and the bridge had been destroyed, the village frightened. The second company took some ten prisoners and lost three men. Four were lightly wounded, and one was taken as prisoner—Zaki. When the company left Yoram saw them pick him up and put him on a truck.

They unloaded equipment and shook hands. It was very early and the Beit-On boys had to walk from the camp to Beit-On.

It feels strange, Nimrod thought, walking, to be so calm and tranquil. Few houses were lighted and the air was brisk and fresh. The sun appeared in all its glory, greeting and drying and warming his body. There were red flowers along the path and Nimrod picked some. He did love flowers. He'd give them to Elli. It was only then that he thought of her, asleep, carrying his child. He didn't feel victorious or glamorous. He felt he had done a job he had to do. He felt dirty and kept picking the flowers, thoughtless, empty-headed. There were some yellow ones, too, and he was aware of the burning pain in his now well-bandaged arm, and the need for a shower, coffee, and some sleep.

He opened the door, quietly. Elli was asleep in the arm-

chair, her hands on her stomach and her yellow hair covering her face.

He passed near her and entered the kitchen, put the
flowers in a vase and, noticing the blood on his hands,
thought how similar the colors were. His gun he put in a
corner, the kettle on the stove, and he started undressing.

"You are wounded!" she screamed, awakening.

"Good morning, sweet one."

She hugged him. "You're wounded," she said again.
"What happened?"

"Just a scratch. We've won it, naturally. The cowards.
They wouldn't even fight, though some were pretty good.
I'm going to take a shower. Here! Some red flowers! The
symbol of blood," he joked.

She could never understand this. Tears came to her eyes
and she moved along into the kitchen.

"I'll tell you all about it, but I'll need some coffee
before, and plenty of hot water to wash away the smells of
the night."

He was singing in the shower, loud, happily, and his
heart was full of love for Elli. He wanted to sleep next to
her warm, clean body.

"Zaki was wounded and taken prisoner," he said from
the shower.

She frowned. "Zaki was taken away? Why Zaki? Why did
they leave him?"

"If I were in his place, I wouldn't mind. It's better than
dying, isn't it, and we had to carry on. I like the boy. He
was so very scared, but he'll be back. I think he spoke your
name. He was in pain and misery but there was nothing I
could do."

It occurred to her he didn't really care but she pushed
the thought away. "If you were in his place," she pondered,

"but you never will be. How can you be scared for others if you don't fear for yourself?" She wanted to talk to Gideon. She wanted Nimrod to be a baby. She wanted her baby to be born and around.

She felt bitterly lonely again and she caught a glimpse of the bunch of red flowers in the new vase. Flowers, red flowers. Symbol of blood. God keep us all.

She felt guilty thinking the way she did and kept herself busy preparing breakfast. She would go to sleep now, next to him, and he was massive and solid and knew better. She was so foolish, she thought. He came out, clean and washed, and stroked her hair, smiling.

## 19

THIS year, the sixth year after the war of liberation, was a good year. The fields turned green early and the crops were good. Nimrod attributed it to the victory in his first battle. But as Yoram said it had started raining since Rina moved to town and, as Zaki was still in jail, nobody was around to say it was God's blessing.

Elli was often sick and very weary. She was expecting in the summer and had another two months to go. More and more often Nimrod had to prepare his own meals and attend to Elli as well, but what worried the family more than all was Miriam's disease. There was nothing the doctors could do or even say. She became smaller and bonier by the day and wouldn't stop working.

"I'm just growing old," she would say, "but will live long enough to help Elli with the child for a long time," and she'd smile.

Then you'd see it. It was a sick smile, very unhealthy and horrid, as if she was slowly losing control of her body and muscles and limbs, and you'd know, as Ivri would, and say, "Yes, Miriam" when counting the days and moments, maybe seconds.

The smells of spring! The green just turning to yellow again and roses in the garden, many roses. The children were on vacation and played "Who is strong?" and the cows gave more milk this year. The border was quiet and while Elli got bigger Miriam was growing smaller by the day.

Miriam seemed lost when in bed, like a baby put in a double bed or, when one entered through the door, like a miniature in a great dark frame, and Nimrod stared into her warm eyes and moved along, always moved along. Few words were spoken, fewer than ever, and something heavy hung in the air, as heavy as sin or guilt. The sun grew warmer, taking the universe into summer, and Miriam was dying. Miriam was dying and only Elli seemed to know it and still have hope. Ivri turned into a shadow, dumb and bent, and Nimrod carried on as if nothing was happening.

"Can we do anything about Mother?" Elli asked.

"Let her die in peace," Nimrod answered.

"How can you talk like this? There must be something we can do. We must at least try."

"I know she's going to die. Very soon," he said, murmuring something to himself, "and she knows it as well. So why cheat and pretend? The woman is eaten from inside. Doctors have given her up. I can't pretend or act, and whenever I look at her, I know that she knows that it's all over. She'll never live to see our child playing in the yard."

Elli became pale, and could hardly stop the scream in her chest.

"How can you talk like this? Your own mother." She was whispering heavily. "You speak as if she were a strange animal. You're killing her faster that way, and Ivri too."

"Hear, hear that! Killing her? What do you want me to

do? Come crying and say 'Mother, you're going to live forever,' say to her not to worry? When I know that every day can be her last, and every bit of spring air might be the last to enter her lungs?"

"Do you love her, Nimrod?"

He didn't answer. "You look pale, kid. Better get to bed and relax. You shouldn't be upset. The child . . ."

"I know, I know. All you care for is the child, as if your mother was but an instrument to produce you and I a means to produce your child. Yes, I'm pale and will go to bed. You know why? Because *I* care, because *I* feel tired, and sick and fed up, because *I* want to look better tomorrow and enjoy the spring air, not because of the child, or you, or anybody."

Nimrod left the room. He did so often now. Whenever their relationship was choked with argument he never explained, or talked or asked. He just left and walked for long hours, kicking stones or whistling a rhythm or playing with grains of sand.

It wasn't death in the air so much as the horrid waiting. Today? The day after? How many rounds would the clock make before she died?

Nimrod realized he had never known his mother well. He would watch her and she was a stranger. She would talk to him, but her voice didn't reach him. He would try to think about her and a sudden meaningless emptiness would master his thoughts, and he gave up.

One morning, when the orange blossoms filled the air and the smell invaded every corner until one's head felt heavy and drunk, Miriam died. Miriam died and Nimrod was away, and nobody knew where he was, or why he wasn't there or when he would be back.

Elli was watching the woman lose her contact with all

that's alive, Ivri looked a mask of despair, and Nimrod was climbing a mountain down south.

Elli had hopes to the last moments. For Ivri something was being cut and scattered among the trees and the odors, and for Nimrod there was the knowledge that this was his mother's last day and he was climbing the mountain, the bare one, the white and wild and wise-looking mountain.

Elli was crying and being sick. Ivri had no tears, and was chased by detailed memories. And Nimrod was meeting death in his own way, challenging nature, taking the hard path and sweating his way up toward some God supposedly resting in the caves on the summit where eagles built their nests and human feet seldom left their marks.

"Where is my son?" the woman asked.

"He'll be here soon," Elli managed to say, weeping.

"No. My son will never be here. My son was never here. He killed Nimi, and Nimrod ran away." She was moaning. She couldn't speak very well. She meant everything she said, and there was guilt in her broken whisper.

Ivri was silent. He thought Nimrod would come, but Elli was losing her balance.

Nimrod was lying to rest halfway up, looking at the cloudless, clear, bluish-white sky and he knew this was the right place to be while his mother was dying. Mother dying? Lamech had died long ago and he hadn't visited the tomb for years. Zaki almost died. Elli would give birth soon. Gideon had been as good as dead for years. And Mother was dying. He could hear the last beats of her heart. He could count the seconds. He knew Elli was crying and he knew Ivri couldn't, and he was there. He got up and walked recklessly on.

A wild pigeon flew away. A stone rolled downhill. Nimrod's feet paused for a second and his hand clutched the canteen. A few drops of sweat appeared on his forehead. His feet hurried on. Elli's eyes were red and her hands shook, Ivri's dumb expression never changed, and Miriam returned her soul to God and her body to dust.

That night Nimrod returned home. Ivri was sitting awaiting him. He was awaiting his son, his past and his future. He was not there in spirit and only there when his son came through the door, flung his bag on the floor, and sat wordlessly to take off his boots. "Are you all right, Ivri?"

"Yes, Nimi. Call me Father. Your mother died without you but then we live without you too. Go, son. Elli is waiting for you in the cottage. I asked her not to stay with me."

Elli was asleep, holding something in her hands and looking as if she were going through a nightmare, face disturbed and distorted, her pregnancy showing through the light cover.

He bent over to kiss her. Elli was holding his leather rabbit, the one Lamech had made, and she was holding it as if it were the last thing to cling to in this world. He touched her hair. "It's all over," he said. And she woke up with a scream. The face she saw was the face of her own son, avoiding her deathbed, and she yelled at him, sobbing, "Get out of here. Go away. I don't want you to touch my child or come near him. Go away, back to your mountain and battles and secret games. Leave me alone."

She got up and entered the bedroom, locking the door behind her. Nimrod approached it. He tried the knob, and then knocked gently. He could hear her sobs, he wanted to talk to her. For a moment he even wanted to bury his head next to the rabbit in her lap, and he knew he couldn't. He had a choking feeling as if an object were stuck all the way down from his mouth through his chest and into his stomach. It wasn't merely a block. It was a pain, and he knew this would last forever, because when he felt things they were down there in his stomach, and when he thought them they were up in his head, and in between was this block and something lacking in the blood, or in the heart or in the veins. And he was helpless as a baby, the Rock opposite a locked door. He couldn't beg or apologize. He couldn't weep or ask. He wanted to tell her how he felt and he was not able to, and he was alone again.

"Look, Elli. Listen to me. Let me in, dear. I knew she was dying. She didn't really want me there, did she? Tell me, did she?

"It's late. Tomorrow is the funeral, and I want you, Elli. Do you hear me? I need you. I say it—I need you. I did love her but don't you see? I had to be alone. Don't you understand? Just my mother and myself and God, and the woman's time came and she had to die. Your time will come to give birth. That's our blessed and horrible life. Aren't you lonely, Elli?"

He fell asleep on the threshold. When he woke to the first beam of sun, he was thinking it was going to be a beautiful day. When he looked around him, his eyes met the rough wooden door and the legs of the chair, and when he looked up the lamp seemed miles away. His body ached and his head was heavy and he went into the kitchen to make some coffee. Another day, just another day.

Ivri just nodded good morning to him and Elli wouldn't talk to him. They took Miriam away to wash her and prepare her and just before noon, an hour during which the lake is utterly unconcerned and the universe indifferent, the small group of people started uphill toward King's Forest and Cemetery Hill, which was covered with a red-and-white carpet of flowers. Gideon could walk slowly, and he was the last in the group. Elli was leaning against Ivri, and Nimrod was leading just behind the coffin. His eyes were dry and he shook the hands stretched toward him in consolation. And the fields were yellowing in the sun below them as if the valley were filled with gold, as if Elli's hair were long enough to cover the whole valley and give it the quality of gold. The freshly dug soil, brown and rich, welcomed them like a hellish well, like a secret entrance into a dark unknown.

Gideon stood next to Nimrod. He exchanged a few words with him and asked about Elli.

"Oh her. She can't understand."

"One day you'll fear death, and then you'll regret a million moments in your life. She doesn't understand, I don't understand, but I know your type of loneliness and this brings us close."

"I will not fear death. Maybe one day I will fear dying. Did you know Miriam well?"

"Did you? Did anybody? Did your father? Maybe her family back in the village near the Volga did. Maybe she's changed since then. We'll never know."

And then the horrid sound of stones and earth being laid and thrown on the corpse, the cruel sound of heavy earth meeting the soft wrapped corpse, one grain after another, counting the years we've still got to live, meeting each other in dumb secrecy, the grains of sand touching one's body like worms or ants—mounting on Gideon's wooden leg, along Elli's belly, and around Nimrod's heart. Around it, never invading it, touching and not entering, surrounding and never ceasing—like a permanent dawn or sunset.

A fresh heap of earth, a cupboard full of simple clay vessels, an empty bed, the handle of the kettle which had almost become a living part of the hand, the emptiness and despair in Ivri's steps, and the long line of people going downhill, the red flowers bowing to them, saying, "We know; we'll see you soon," and the rocks whispering, "You'll all be brought here."

Nimrod walked the long way back to the white valley and through the narrow path down to the village.

When he climbed the stairs he wondered where Elli had put the rabbit. He entered the living room, opened the kitchen door, and walked into the bedroom.

Elli's things were scattered in unusual disorder and he could feel her absence.

"Elli! Elli!" His voice was strong and hoarse, changing into a bitter cry and then a whisper. He knew she was gone.

He walked slowly as if avoiding a hidden danger. He locked the door behind him and looked for Ivri.

"Elli is gone," he said to him.

"I know, son. I saw her leaving."

"Why didn't you stop her? You saw my wife leaving, carrying your grandson, and you let her go?"

"I saw Elli, a woman, leaving, and I let her go. I see my son opposite me, wrong, and I tell him to go after her."

Nimrod left his father, went back to the house, and lay on the bed. Not meaning to, he fell asleep, his hand moving in vain, as a matter of habit, looking for Elli's warm body.

# 20

"I'LL open it," Yoram said to Rina. They were sitting in their modern Tel Aviv apartment, and it was late in the evening. The door to the terrace was open and one could hear the soft sound of the waves and breathe in the mixture of fresh air with the salty smells of the sea and the city.

"It seems strange that someone would come over this late," said Rina turning her head toward the door.

The woman who entered seemed a stranger for a second. She was heavily pregnant, her yellow hair disheveled and long, and there was a deep look of misery in her red swollen eyes.

Elli had been weeping the whole day. Her legs looked red and heavy and she sank into the armchair offered to her by Yoram, and couldn't talk. The tears covered her cheeks and neck and hung on her collar, and she couldn't speak. She was shivering and shaking and holding her stomach and all her body was trying to say something.

"Please put out the lights. I can't stand it," she whispered. Rina did, and put the kettle on.

"Here, sweet, relax. You'll have some tea and a hot bath and you can sleep some and we'll talk in the morning. Would you like my doctor to come over?"

"I don't care."

"Shall we let Nimrod know you are here? He'll be worried, probably looking for you?"

"Nimrod," she said, as if in a dream, her eyes wandering into the distant darkness. "Nimrod . . . no, Nimrod is asleep. Never call Nimrod. Maybe I'll call on Miriam tonight—but Miriam was buried today."

"Yes, dear. We know. We couldn't come because Rina didn't feel well."

"Nimrod didn't come either," she laughed. "He says all old women die. He says she didn't want him there. Nimrod killed her." She laughed louder, and was shivering. Yoram shut the glass door leading to the terrace.

"Open the doors," she screamed. "I'll choke. It's so hot in here. Open the tombs and the doors and the wombs or we'll all choke." She was crying and laughing now. "Why talk in the morning when there is nothing to say? Can a rock love, or cry or care or want things? I love him," she wept. "I married a stone, a trunk of a tree which died when it was born, a wild valley where nothing grows. I don't want my baby, Rina. Do you hear that? I don't want my baby." She moved her elbow and it struck the glass of tea ready for her. The glass fell and broke on the floor. The sound of breaking glass, sudden and metallic, electrified her, and she stopped weeping. Her scream changed into a whisper. "I don't want the baby. I want my father. I don't want anybody. Please leave me alone," and whispering and murmuring she fell asleep on the chair. Yoram and Rina moved her to the bed and gently covered her weary body.

"What is the matter?" Yoram asked.

"I understand it all," said Rina, hiding a tear. "Let's go to sleep. She'll be all right now. I know what she means." And she hugged Yoram gently and gratefully as she had never done before.

They did call Nimrod, and asked him not to come for a few days. "She'll relax and return home. Right now she's all worked up and her nerves are strained."

"But the baby?"

"She'll see Rina's doctor. Don't worry. Rina is taking care of her and I think it's good that way. It will give you time to think."

"Yoram, why did she leave like that? I think I'm a beast, but then I know she loves me. I can't change anything."

"She left because when a woman doubts whether her husband has a heart she leaves. She keeps talking about her father. She's lonely, Nimrod. Did it ever occur to you?"

"We all are. I'll wait for her . . ."

Elli's condition didn't improve. She was detached and tired, didn't listen or answer or ask, and kept repeating the same few words. . . . "I don't want the baby. . . . I want to see my father. . . . I married a stone. . . ." And she would talk to herself in Hungarian for many hours. Whenever Nimrod's name was mentioned, her face froze, adopting a peculiar expression—half smile, half detestation—and she would automatically touch her belly.

The doctor saw her, and gave her a few injections. "It's the nerves and the mind," he said. "She ought to go home. I'd send her husband to the doctor."

In Beit-On life continued flowing in the path of summer labors, approaching harvest, a heat wave, whispering gossiping tongues, and glasses of tea on terraces late at night. The villagers said Elli was not herself since Miriam died. Ivri said it was a good change for her to be with Rina in town, and he seldom talked to Nimrod, who kept himself busy on the farm, calling Yoram at times to ask when Elli would come home.

Nimrod did try to understand, for he missed Elli. He went to Haifa one morning to choose things for the house and the baby, and he walked for hours along the main streets, inexperienced, troubled, and lost. The trip ended by his buying a new plough, some steel nails, a toy he thought he liked which by the time he came home he didn't any more, and a new blanket for Elli which he knew she wanted and liked as she had pointed it out to him when they were last in town.

Nimrod tried but he didn't get very far. He realized how many were the things he took for granted, and felt the absence of Elli when she was away, and he called this feeling love. It always seemed to him superfluous to put into words his love or emotions as he never demanded this from other people, but as he was puzzled and rather upset he thought it right to visit Gideon and try to solve it together. Perhaps even Gideon should talk to Elli.

Something had happened to Gideon since he last saw him at the funeral. To those easily fooled it seemed as if he had improved. He looked fatter and healthier, but one could see something new in his eyes and smile, something not quite sane and regular which was above the bitterness and sorrow and cynicism. And Nimrod saw it, and regretted coming the moment Gideon opened the door.

"Elli is gone." Gideon smiled. "Miriam is gone. Ivri is gone, and I'll be going soon. And you were never here anyway."

"What are you talking about?"

"It's the climate, you see, this lovely little village on the

lake. It's not so easy to leave it all behind and call yourself
new. It takes a slow, slow process and we are all dead because we hurry to swallow the bread before chewing it, so
we strangle ourselves. I knew Elli would leave, but she'll
come back if that's what you are worried about."

"How did you know?"

"Because the fool loves you. And in spite of all, she loves
in you the new and the nauseating and the strong and the
stony and she faced it until now and will come back to it.
You make me sick, man. It's a good country. It doesn't eat
its inhabitants, but we eat ourselves. True, you are not
alone, but then are not all like that?"

"Have you seen Ivri? He worries me. I want to help
him."

"No you don't. You think he's a fool. He's worried? It's
guilt. I feel the same way. We fed you with sand and
now when the grains have united we wonder why you
throw up stones instead of cream cakes. When will your
child be born?"

"In a couple of months. If it's a boy, Elli wants him to be
called Gideon. She likes you very much. That's why I came
over here."

"Yes, that's why. Do you want the child?"

"Are you joking? Do I want the child? This is only the
first one!"

"Aren't you scared of having a child? What if he ends
your way, or mine?"

"I'd like him to. My father wanted me to be different
from himself, and I want my son to be like me. And, of
course, if it's a girl, I want her to be like Elli—but that's
obvious."

"Nimi, can I ask you a favor?"

"Please, anything."

"Go now, this moment, to Yoram and Rina, and bring your wife home. I know she'll be willing."

"All right, I will. I suppose that's the thing to do." Nimrod was about to leave the room when he heard Gideon.

"Yes, one more thing!"

"What is it?"

"Don't ever come back here, not as long as I live, but ask Elli to pass by for an hour when she can make it. I have a message for her."

Nimrod didn't answer. He left the house and was sure now that Gideon was slowly going out of his mind. He knew there was no point in discussing it or asking or explaining, and he measured the unpaved road to his house with wide violent steps, packed a bag, and walked to the main road to catch the bus to Tel Aviv. . . .

He walked up the stairs, pressed the door bell, and went in. Elli was knitting and Yoram was talking to Rina.

"Shalom." He kissed Elli, who remained silent. "We're going home, sweetheart. Can you pack quickly? I know a husband of yours who can't do without you and I thought it'd be a good idea if you'd come over and see for yourself!" He was smiling and looked kind and pleasant and loving.

"It'll take a few moments," Elli said, and left the room. Rina offered him coffee. Yoram asked about the farm. No one wanted to ask or be asked delicate questions.

"She'll be all right," Rina said. "My doctor took care of her and very soon you'll be very happy parents."

"I'm glad you came over," Yoram said. "She was going to return tomorrow anyway. She spent a few days at the archives looking for her father's name."

"Did she find anything?"

"Not that we know of, but it's all very strange as she refuses to talk about it, and we didn't want to press the point."

"Take care of her, Nimrod. She is so precious and fragile and easily hurt, and there are many things you don't know or understand."

Elli entered the room with a curious smile.

"Let's go home," she said. "I've missed it, but I had to go and come back, you know. I had to find my father." He knew she didn't want to be asked questions.

They say a light in Ivri's window. "Ivri, Elli is back. Come and have breakfast with us in the morning," Nimrod said through the window.

"Every morning," Elli added, and they climbed the stairs to their house, to the bedroom where Elli started unpacking while Nimrod took a shower. She noticed the blanket, and couldn't help the tears. She was lying on the bed, clutching the blanket, and crying, "Why can't he always be like that?" and she knew he wanted to and couldn't and almost resigned herself to it. And her love for him was mixed with pity.

They lay awake.

"The baby is kicking hard now," she said. "I can feel it all the time." She took his large rough hand and put it on her belly. He noticed a movement, and kept his hand there.

"Yes, the baby is moving. Are you proud, Mother?"

She frowned. "He's been moving and kicking and hurting and I love you so much," she whispered. He felt it all, the kicking and the pain, and the love. He wished it could all happen inside his body. He was almost jealous.

"Nimrod, my father died six years ago."

He sat up. "How do you know? Why didn't you tell me?"

"I checked. He died in a hospital here. He had a bad disease he got in a camp. They couldn't do anything to save him. I feel better now; at least I know. It's the uncertainty which was painful. But I didn't expect to find him. I knew he was dead and thought of him as dead, but I had to find out. Let's not talk about it."

"I saw Gideon today. He wants you to come over. He doesn't want to see me ever again."

"I know. He called me the other day. He sent me some poems. They frightened me."

"Why?"

"They are all about flowers about to die, and plants that should die to give room to others, and there is something new and horrible in his poems and voice—as if he has a date with death, which he intends to keep, and accepts, and this is not normal. I'm so frightened."

"Here, come nearer, dear. We've had a hard time but everything is fine now. You know it is. Tell me you do."

"Yes, I do. And next month or so there will be the three of us, and it'll make Ivri feel better too. And I have so many plans for the future, and it's so good to have you back. I only wish I could understand."

"Stop it. It's no use. Please, let's sleep."

She fell fast asleep.

A few hours later she woke up. "Nimrod?"

"Yes, Elli."

"You have been awake all the time, haven't you?"

"Yes, Elli."

"Tell me, do you think my child will be near me when I die?"

The question hovered somewhere above the bed, unanswered. He touched her belly again to feel the movement inside it. She put her hand on his. She didn't really expect him to answer. He put his hand on her shoulder and held her breast, he stroked her body. He wanted to tell her they would all be there if she died but he wasn't sure himself. Perhaps they'd be climbing the mountain, or fighting a war. Perhaps they'd all be there. He couldn't say.

"Sleep, baby," he said, and she did. He watched the new day's light through the half-closed shutters.

## 21

ELLI was to go to the hospital in Poria, near Tiberias, which was the best around. Everything was ready for the baby and the atmosphere seemed to be relaxed and easy. Ivri smiled more often, and though he would walk to Miriam's tomb every Saturday morning it looked as if he were getting used to being alone. Elli suffered from the heat and wished it were all over and Nimrod was the happiest of all. Rina gave birth in Tel Aviv to a girl and nobody seemed to remember the agony and despair Elli had gone through after Miriam's death. Elli did go to see Gideon once and told Nimrod nothing about it—just a few more poems she said.

One Sunday morning she was taken to the hospital and things happened fast in Beit-On.

Nimrod was told he was to stay behind as it would be a few days before the actual birth. Elli begged him not to come along, and she was taken in the doctor's car. Nimrod saw her off and he came home to find Ivri awaiting him, pale and shaking. "Here," he said. "A letter for you."

There was an envelope on which the name Nimrod was written, and it looked heavy.

"Who from?"

"Your friend Gideon. He's dead."

Nimrod turned to run when Ivri's hand stopped him. "Don't. It looks horrible. He did it with a shot in the stomach and one in the head. He left only this letter for you. I knew he'd end like this. There was no point for him in carrying on, he thought. I waited for it for months and days and now it's happened. Don't let Elli know until she comes back with the baby. It'll be a terrible shock for her."

Nimrod went to Gideon's house. A few people were gathered around the door and in the corridor and Nimrod pushed his way in. A lump of a man, the remains of a being, a leftover of a leftover of a body was thrown in the middle of the perfectly clean and cool room. The wooden leg was separated from the body, lonely and accusing, the eyes shut, the lips turned down in an expression of intangible sorrow and sadness, and more blood than anybody thought Gideon's body contained was spattered and pooled around the corpse. The gun was next to the hand and the scene was so unlike Beit-On, so strangely foreign in this very hot summer morning that you wouldn't think it was true. Nimrod nodded and pushed his way out. "Poor man," people whispered. "We knew he'd end this way. . . . Well, he wasn't quite sane was he? . . . He used to be called the Rock. . . ."

For the first time in many years Nimrod wanted to weep, and there was nobody to weep with. Miriam was dead and Elli was away and not to be informed. And the loss of Gideon became larger than life and he couldn't comprehend it. Pictures and glimpses from childhood floated and reached his conscience and faded again and he walked to the old meeting place, past the pink house, ran across the field, to the white valley which looked whiter than ever, and there he opened the envelope.

"Nimi dear," it started. "I wanted to write you a million lines, but words never went deep into you, so why waste them. Still, here are some in the form of a good-by. I am going to die the day Elli goes to the hospital. I am going to die anyway, and as I was dead for many years it's only a change of place, a few feet above or under our rich brown soil, not really much more.

"When your wife came to me a few months ago and said the doctor suggested it might be dangerous for her to have the child, I was again the Rock. I was once more the devil who mocked you for your curly hair and slow movement, and I advised her not to tell you. More than that, I told her to have the baby and risk it. Do you realize what that means? I said she'd never be happy if she didn't give you children. I said it would kill you. I said that as the chance was fifty-fifty she should have it. I told her not to tell you, and she knew how well I knew you, and she loves you more than she loves life. The truth is that you don't deserve even a shadow of a sacrifice and I am an insane fool. The truth is that it was haunting me and driving me, and whatever will happen I can't face so I choose this as an excuse to do something I want to do anyway and couldn't before because I am a coward.

"I always felt guilty about you. I know I killed the good in you—the fear. I set a wrong example. I killed you because I was killed in the same way earlier and this was an easy revenge. And then it was too late and you wouldn't listen.

"My life was a misery. I never felt things to the end. I

never cared for anybody. I never understood anybody. I was alone in my strength and physical wisdom and when it was all gone I joyed in seeing you going through the same machine, losing and gaining the same qualities, and I still loved you because I was rotten, strong and rotten, and then weak and rotten. It takes great courage to be afraid, and we don't have this kind of courage. So I end here and you are doomed to tread on this earth with this load of in-human, ugly fearlessness until you die. And in the process you'll dry and kill and abolish all around you—your parents, wife, children, and more than all, yourself. And when you're dying and looking back you'll see I was right, and you'll regret all the tears you couldn't shed, all the tenderness you didn't pour out, all the fears you never experienced, and all the poems you never lived through, as your life is an essay not a poem. And when my life did become a poem it was one of self-pity, and an ugly de-formed one.

"I couldn't face the possibility of Elli hurting herself because of me, or your hatred when you found out, but there are excuses.

"Carry on, little boy. Climb the mountains and plough the fields and have children. Let them be scared, Nimrod. Let them play with dolls, don't let them be the newer type. Don't make them into rocks, as the rock is the loneliest among all. Maybe you've understood me always. Maybe you never will. I leave this world now, and I'll join the better ones, the ones we kill, the Lamechs and the Miriams, and if you have a God, boy, pray to him to have pity of you. Gideon."

Nimrod rushed to the main road, and in half an hour reached the hospital. He was told to wait and after two hours a nurse dressed in very starched white came out.

"Nimrod? From Beit-On?"

"Yes. Me!"

"A son was born to you. Your wife is very weak and will need a good rest. I suppose you knew it would be a dangerous operation, but it's over now. The child is healthy and fine. You can return home. You'll be able to see them tomorrow."

A tall man left the Poria hospital. He looked older and bent and there was a flat expression of gratefulness and worry in his eyes. Nimrod went home.

"Father," he said to Ivri. "Father—you have a grandson Gideon. We'll call him Gidi. We'll pay a visit to Elli and my son tomorrow."

He climbed the stairs home, put the letter in the drawer, and kept saying, "If I had a God I'd pray to him. I don't know any God but I have a son."

The next day they went to visit the mother and son. Elli was smiling, a clean, healthy, relaxed smile, and Nimrod bent down to kiss her. When Ivri left the room, he looked her in the eyes and asked, "Why didn't you tell me?"

"Tell you what?"

"It was dangerous, the nurse told me. You should have let me know!"

"And have us both worried and troubled? I felt I'd be all right. I asked Gideon. He was very clever and good about it. And you see he was right! He'll be very happy. Does he know we have a son and I'm all right?"

"Yes, Elli, I suppose he knows."

"We'll name him Gideon won't we?"

"Yes, Elli. We will. Was it dreadful?"

She lowered her eyes. "I was so scared. I went to pieces millions of times. And then I didn't feel anything, and then they brought him in and I couldn't believe it was all over, and we had a son. You wanted a boy very much, didn't you?"

"Well, yes, to say the truth. The next one had better be a girl, though."

She shivered. "There will be no next one, Nimrod. You'd better know. They had to operate to get this one out and I can't have any more children." She was crying now.

"Here, here, sweet. Don't. Don't now."

He held her head between his hands. "You shouldn't think of it now. We have a son. After all, I was an only child too. Three make a large family. Don't. Please. . . ."

The nurse entered the room. "Do you want to see the boy? You can stay for a few more minutes when he's brought in, and then leave. You can come again tomorrow."

Another nurse brought in the child. "My son," the pulse in Nimrod's throat was beating. "My own little boy." True, he looked like all babies, red, fuzzy-haired, wrinkled, all wrapped and packaged, but it was his Gideon, his boy, and he wanted so much to take him home now and take Elli home, and be alone, the three of them, when he remembered Gideon. No, he couldn't tell her, not yet anyway. He'd never show her the letter. She wouldn't be able to take it. Never. . . .

"Anything wrong, Nimrod?"

"No. He's beautiful. I'm so excited! When can you two come home?"

"In a couple of days. I think you ought to go now. Take care of yourself. It won't be long. And please, go and see Gideon. He'll be very happy, I know."

Ivri was waiting outside the hospital. They were both thinking about Gideon.

"I can't tell her, Ivri. I just won't be able to."

"What was in the letter, son?"

"I don't know. Many things, some made sense and some didn't. He wasn't completely sane. He didn't know what he was doing."

"Are you sure?"

"No, not really, but I can't tell Elli. Will you?"

"No, son. You'll have to. There is no other way. And she won't forgive you if you aren't the one to tell her. But you've got a few days to think about it."

"Do you like the boy?"

"Yes, of course. But he brings back sad memories. I remember when you were born we had hard times. All was so different then. Your boy will have it easier, I suppose. It feels old to be a grandfather, and I know how anxious Miriam was to raise her grandchildren. She longed to have them, and now. . . ." Ivri withdrew into his silence and mask of sorrow which sealed him off completely. They spent the rest of the day working on the farm, sweating out their thoughts and anxieties and dreams and memories.

Two days later Nimrod went to Poria to bring Elli and Gidi home.

The child was a miracle for Nimrod. It moved, it had ten fingers. Later he started smiling. He learned to turn over and he was so alive. He was screaming, wanting things, and he was his son. The first year in Gidi's life was a good one for all of them. Elli recovered from the shock of Gideon's death and was too busy with the child to think about other things. The farm was enlarged and they made plans for rebuilding the cottage. Nimrod hadn't changed, but by caring for the child some new lines of kindness and gentleness were drawn on his rough character. And as for Ivri, his life now centered around the baby.

Things started becoming difficult when Elli and Nimrod

began talking about the child's future. Nimrod took his future for granted. There was no need to plan or think about it. He was going to be Father's boy. He would go to school in the village and work on the farm. He would learn to love the country, know it, and defend it and he would be happy in the way Nimrod considered himself happy. Elli thought otherwise. She wanted Gidi to have a childhood. She wanted him to be spoiled as long as he could, to learn to live with people and love them, and not isolate himself. And while the baby was asleep in his cradle, his parents were arguing about what would be best for him. Elli gave up. She didn't, really, but she couldn't explain it all to Nimrod as he would ask, "Do you love me?" And as she answered yes, he'd say, "Well, then, you want Gidi to be like me, don't you?" "No," she'd say and he'd be angry and ask her to explain. She couldn't explain and she'd go into the small room and stare at Gideon for many minutes, stroking his dark hair and listening to his breathing.

When the baby was three years old the war broke out with Egypt. Nimrod volunteered and went down south, to the Sinai Peninsula.

"Where is daddy going?"

"On a trip," said Elli. Nimrod took the child and explained it to him.

"Daddy is going to war."

"What is war?"

"You see this sword on the wall? Well, we fight with guns. Boom!"

The child was scared now and his lips turned down ready to cry.

"Here, Gideon. Come. Don't cry. I'll be back soon."

"Will you bring me something from your trip, Daddy?"

"What do you want, son?"

"A toy."

"There are no toys in the war, only swords and guns. Boom!"

The boy was frightened again, and Elli angrily took him out of the room.

The war was short and the men were drunk with the fast victory. They swept through the wilderness of the Sinai Peninsula where thousands of shoes were scattered and the crows flew above corpses. The land was new and the people at first too tense and then too relaxed. And when Nimrod came back home he was again the Rock, with his war stories, with the excitement of a child over new gifts, and he was only sorry that his son was too small to understand his stories and enthusiasm. "One day I'll tell him what it feels like. He'll be very proud one day, as Ivri was when I climbed the mountain."

"It can wait," Elli said. "Yes it surely can wait."

When the boy was four, Nimrod had an unpleasant quarrel with Ivri about him. Ivri was now the storyteller, and one evening Nimrod stopped near the window and listened to one of his stories. It was about the Rabbi, Ivri's father, about how he used to beat Ivri and about the Volga which is ten times wider than the Jordan. How funny it all was. It was a story about Miriam, and a fairy tale in addition. The boy was happily laughing, following the story, asking and inventing on his own. Later that night, when Gidi was in bed, Nimrod went to see his father.

"I heard your story today, Ivri. You seem to have changed. You used to tell me different stories."

"You didn't listen. You never liked them. I wonder if you remember a man named Lamech?"

For a moment no words were spoken. "Yes, I remember Lamech," Nimrod said. "You cut him out of my life. You said he was harmful and dangerous and above all a fool."

"It was my mistake. I'm trying not to repeat it with my grandson."

"Mistake? You mean to say your life was a mistake? Miriam's too? And am I a mistake? You said it was good for me to see Gideon and not Lamech. Now they are both dead, and who knows? Nothing would make me happier than if my son became like me. That would not be a mistake, and after all, I am his father."

"But we don't need that kind of life any more. It's all changed now."

"Did we need it then?" There was bitterness in his last question and Nimrod left the house. The boy was asleep, quiet and calm and handsome. And this was all that mattered. When he saw the child he almost felt sorry he had been rude to Ivri. He kissed Gidi and went out for a walk.

## 22

SEVERAL years passed by, the borders were quiet after the Sinai victory, and Beit-On became wealthier. It was spring again. Gidi was in his first year at school, his hair became darker and his eyes brighter, and he did become Father's boy.

He came back from school earlier one day, at the beginning of the holiday, flung his books in a corner, took off his shirt, and was ready to go out.

"Gidi, where to?" Elli asked him when Nimrod entered the room.

"Don't call him Gidi," Nimrod said. "He doesn't like to be nicknamed any more. My young lad, Gideon."

"We're meeting for a game, Father. Shalom." He left.

The secret meeting place was down near the river now, and Igal was the leader. Winter was stamp-collecting time and spring was when the children of Beit-On played the secret game "Who is strong?" Gidi was the youngest in the group, but was accepted because his father was the best fighter in the village and because he would choose very difficult tasks.

The children were seated in a circle. The warm sun stroked them gently and the lake was shining very near. The Jordan was singing its perpetual hymn to nature, flowing down from the Chermon into the lake, ending somewhere in the Dead Sea where the life it brought died in the heat and the salt.

Igal would get up and ask, "Who is strong?" And the children would rise one by one and say, "I am strong," generation after generation, year after year.

Gidi could swim well, but the stream was strong this day and cold and he thought he should choose something else. But his turn hadn't come yet and he occupied himself by watching the spring birds and encouraging his friends.

Nimrod went down to the lake and thought he'd take the long way back, walking along the river and climbing the path up to the hill of Beit-On.

It was Gideon's turn now. He got up and said with confidence, "I am strong." The chorus of many voices followed, "Show us you are strong!" He could hear the echo from the river rolling and humming and struggling through bushes and rocks and trunks. "Show me you are strong." The lake smiled back quietly demanding "Show me you are strong!" So did the highest trees and the deepest waters and the cloudless spring clean sky, and the children asked, "What will you do?"

He changed his mind, as all seemed so tranquil and peaceful. "I'll swim across the river!" The children rushed down. He took off his slacks and sandals and remained in his underwear. "I'll swim there—and back!" he screamed, and dived in. The stream was very strong, and the waves and the foam and the drops stroking and smoothing his little body were saying, "Show us you're strong." And he knew Nimrod would like him to swim there and back, when Nimrod suddenly appeared!

All Nimrod could see was the small head, appearing and disappearing under the current, and for a second, or one-tenth of a second which seemed like years, the little head didn't appear.

Something went wrong. Everything went wrong. The Rock was scared. Nimi, Nimrod, the fighter, the new type, was scared stiff. The feeling was new and he couldn't sense anything but this fear. There was an overcoming, paralyzing fear. He couldn't move, or shout or do anything. He was rooted to his spot, and his legs and hands seemed to be separated from his body. His heart stopped beating and he was bathed in sweat. All the fears that had been hidden and drowned and murdered were now pushing their way through, mocking and conquering and invading. All the moments—all the highest trees and mountains, the being alone in the cemetery, the heights of battles—they were all there.

He jumped into the sounding waters. He could hardly swim, or sense or feel. This was his son, drowning, and he loved him as he had never loved him before, as he had never loved anything before really, and then his hand touched the little head and the father and son were on the other side of the roaring river.

"Daddy! You spoiled everything! We're playing the game. You know." Gideon looked at his father. He had never seen him like that. The whites of his eyes were whiter than ever and his hands were shaking. He clutched the boy to his chest and started weeping. It was a sorrowful cry like the words first spoken by a mute man. He didn't know how to cry well and he was shivering and kissing the boy and stroking his wet hair and kissing him again.

"My son, Gidi. Are you all right? We'll go home to Mother, now." He was on his knees, wet and cold and frightened. The Rock broke, and it broke into a thousand pieces.

"Are you sick, Daddy?" Gidi was ashamed. All the children were watching. His father, the fighter, weeping. His father, the Rock, didn't let him show he was strong.

"I want to go home," he said. "I'm sleepy."

Nimrod couldn't speak. He took the child on his back and swam across the river, held his hand, and walked with him through the village to the house. The boy was still ashamed. Nimrod was weeping and couldn't control the tears and the people were watching and whispering. But the man was happy. He could cry, and love, and sing. He was afraid and full of feeling, and a new unknown warmth which was human and tender swept over him in a way he never had known before.

They arrived home. Nimrod kissed Elli, on the lips, on her cheeks and neck and breast, and lifted her high up in the air.

"Nimrod. What is it? Something is wrong. Please tell me! Stop it. The child is watching!"

"Let him watch. His father loves his mother. Let him watch." And Gideon looked up and said five bitter accusing words, "Mother, Daddy is a coward."

There was silence. The boy started crying and went into his room. Elli followed him and Nimrod went to look for Ivri. Ivri was in the cowshed. Nimrod went toward him, tears still in his eyes, and he cried gently on his shoulder.

"Cry, boy. Cry, little child," Ivri said. He understood. There was no need to speak or explain. He had understood for years. "It can't be too late," he said. "Go talk to your son. Call him Gidi and tell him Lamech's stories, and love, love it all. And suffer and love that too. Go, my boy, pray to God. And talk to your son."

Gidi was on his bed. He was not crying now but he didn't move when Nimrod entered the room.

"I don't want to see you, Daddy," he said.

"I've got something for you, boy, and I want to talk to you."

The boy turned around. "A gift?"

"Yes, boy. Just one moment!" Nimrod left the room and went into the bedroom. In the drawer, among Elli's belongings, there was the rabbit. It looked like anything but a rabbit but it was his rabbit, the beautiful toy Lamech had made of leather. And he took it, clutching it as if it were his last hope. The ears were fallen and the seams undone and some of the stuffing was showing. One eye was missing, but it was his rabbit.

He brought it to his son. "Here, boy, a toy! A funny rabbit. I'll tell you its story. It's a long, long story. Maybe the longest you've ever heard!"

"I am not a baby, Nimrod," Gideon said looking him straight in the eyes. "I don't want a toy. You promised me a pocketknife, like Igal's. I'm sleepy now."

"Don't you want to hear a story?"

"No, Father. I don't like stories very much."

Everything was dark, darker than it had ever been before. The big man left his house. He had broken the shell and was hurt, and helpless and lost. Elli was beloved, but a stranger. Ivri was depressed. And his son wanted a pocketknife. He walked slowly and then faster, past the pink house, into the wood, up the hill, and through the new gate to the cemetery. There he was alone. It was not the loneliness of the strong and superior. It was the loneliness of the weak and helpless. There was Lamech, singing a song, his beard dirty and gray. There was Miriam, Mother, wrinkled and bent and old and loving. And Gideon, the warrior, just outside the fence, with his wooden leg and book of poems. These who had died. And if he was the living among the dead ones, he had died a sudden death today and was doomed to live among the dead ones.

All of a sudden he could hear sounds and voices, the stories Lamech used to tell, his mother calling him Nimi, Zaki's wounded voice yelling, "Don't leave me alone," Elli moaning, Gideon preaching, "You'll kill all around you and above all you'll kill yourself." He could hear the lake and the river and the highest trees. They were not saying, "Show us you are strong." They were saying, "We're beautiful, love us," and the universe echoed, "Love me," but he could see he was at the bottom, where you belong when "you always choose the wrong," as Lamech had said, and the ladder was taken away. There was nobody to answer him. He was jealous of those who had lived when he was asleep and frightened of those who were still asleep around him. He lay on the grass shaken and tired and next to the bed in his son's room lay the rabbit staring at the ceiling with his one eye, neglected, unwanted, but superior.

# ABOUT THE AUTHOR

Yaël Dayan was born on February 12, 1939, in Nahahal, a village of some eighty families near Haifa. Her parents and grandparents were also born in the land that is now Israel. The villagers lived in a climate of danger, and when there wasn't a real war there was always tension and, not far away, the border. Yaël Dayan contributed her earliest writings to Israeli youth magazines while in high school, and attended the University of Jerusalem's School of Political Science for three years. She then went to London where she wrote for the *Jewish Observer* and the Hebrew Program for the BBC. Yaël Dayan has traveled throughout western Europe and the Scandinavian countries; she made a lecture tour of the United States for Israel Bonds when she was seventeen, again in 1959, when her first book was published, and has agreed to return for yet another tour of lectures early in 1961. When the Sinai war broke out in 1956, she returned immediately from America to enlist in the Israeli Army. After basic training, she entered the cadet school and became a lieutenant. Her first novel, *New Face in the Mirror*, was written mostly during off-duty hours and long night watches as an officer in her two years' service in the Army. *Envy the Frightened* was written in Greece, where Miss Dayan spends a few months every year. Although Hebrew is her mother tongue, she speaks several languages fluently; she writes her novels in English and translates them into Hebrew. Yaël Dayan is the daughter of General Moshe Dayan, former Commander in Chief of the Israeli Army and now Minister of Agriculture, and Ruth Dayan, who directs "Maskit," home-industries project. She grew up in Israel in a tightly knit family group which includes two younger brothers, Udi, three years younger, and Assi, now 15—to whom this book is dedicated.

This book was set in

Baskerville type by

The Haddon Craftsmen.

It was printed and bound at

the press of The World Publishing Company.

Design is by Larry Kamp.